the GIRL and the GHOST

ALKAF

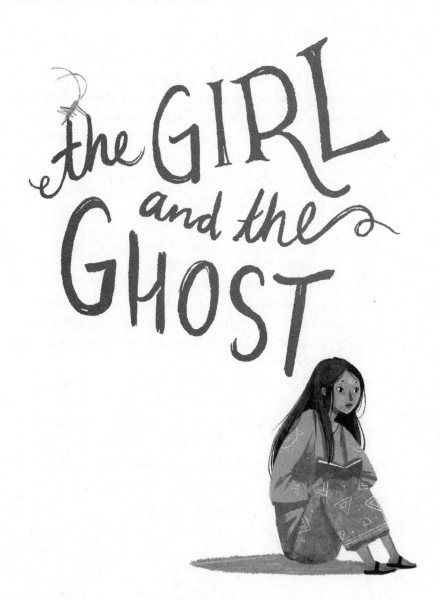

the GIRL
and the
GHOST

HARPER

An Imprint of HarperCollins*Publishers*

Library of Congress Cataloging-in-Publication Data

Names: Hanna Alkaf, author.

Title: The girl and the ghost / Hanna Alkaf.

Description: First edition. | New York, NY : Harper, [2020] | Audience: Ages 8–12. | Audience: Grades 4–6. | Summary: Retells a Malaysian folk tale in which a lonely girl, Suraya, inherits from her grandmother a pelesit, a ghostly demon, who proves to be a good companion, bringing both danger and hope.

Identifiers: LCCN 2019040567 | ISBN 978-0-06-294095-7 (hardcover)

Subjects: CYAC: Demonology—Fiction. | Friendship—Fiction. | Single-parent families—Fiction. | Mothers and daughters—Fiction. | Muslims—Fiction.| Malaysia—Fiction.

Classification: LCC PZ7.1.H36377 Gir 2020 | DDC [Fic]—dc23

LC record available at https://lccn.loc.gov/2019040567

Typography by Alice Wang

21 22 23 24 PC/LSCH 10 9 8 7 6 5 4 3 2

First Edition

*For the kids who are afraid—whether it's of
bullies or ghosts or grumpy moms, first days or bad
days or everything in-between days.
You have more courage than you know.
(And for Malik and Maryam,
because every book I ever write is for you.)*

PROLOGUE

THE GHOST KNEW his master was about to die, and he wasn't exactly unhappy about it.

He knew that sounded bad. You'd think, after all those years together, that even he might have felt a twinge of sadness about the whole situation. But it's hard to feel sorry for someone when: a) you're a ghost, and everyone knows ghosts don't have hearts, and b) that someone made her living out of forcing you to make other people miserable.

He stared at her now as she lay on the narrow bed, gray and gaunt in the light of the full moon, her breath rasping and shallow. Watching her teeter slowly toward the end was a bit like watching a grape slowly become a raisin: the years had sucked the life and vitality out of her until she was nothing but a wrinkled shell of her former self.

"Well," she wheezed, squinting at him.

Well, he said.

"One more for the road, eh?" she said, nodding to the full moon out the window. And she grimaced as she offered him the ring finger of her right hand, as she had done so many times before.

The ghost nodded. It seemed frivolous, but after all, he still needed to eat, whether or not his master lay dying. As he bent his head over the wrinkled hand, his sharp little teeth pricking the skin worn and calloused from time and use, the witch let out a sharp breath. Her blood used to be rich and strong and so thick with her magic that the ghost could get himself drunk on it, if he wasn't careful. Now all he tasted was the stale tang of age, the sour notes that came with impending death, and a bitter aftertaste he couldn't quite place. Regret, perhaps.

It was the regret that was hardest to swallow.

The ghost drank nothing more than he had to, finishing quickly and sealing the tiny pinpricks of his teeth on her skin with spit. *It is done,* he told her, the words familiar as a favorite song, the ritual as comforting as a warm blanket. *And I am bound to you, until the end.*

The witch patted his horned head gently. Her touch surprised him—she had never been particularly affectionate.

"Well," she said, her voice nothing more than a sigh. "The end is now."

And she turned her head to the window, where the sun was just rising over the cusp of the world, and died.

ONE

ghost

FOR A WHILE after the witch drew her final breath the ghost sat very still, wondering what to do next. Theoretically, he knew what was supposed to happen: he was a pelesit after all, and a pelesit must have a master. And since he was bound by blood, his new master had to be of the same blood as the old.

It was finding this new blood that was going to be tricky. The witch had not been much for family. Or friends. Or, if he was being completely honest, people in general. There was a daughter, he knew, a little girl with lopsided pigtails and an equally lopsided grin. He had seen pictures of her, pictures the witch kept hidden in a drawer among bits of broken candles, coupons for supermarket deals long expired, a small mountain of coins: things she no longer had use for, or that weighed her down; things she had forgotten or wanted to forget. There were letters too, slanted words written in deep blue ink, the paper old enough that yellow age stains had started to blossom at the edges:

I know you don't approve, but he loves me and I love him, and we want to be together.

We have our own home now, wouldn't you like to come and visit us?

Please write to me, Mama. I miss you. Won't you want to see your grandchild?

The last one was newer, a rectangle of plain white tucked into a crinkly brown envelope bearing the witch's name. It said: *Do not contact us again.*

No, the old witch wasn't much for family; instead she roamed from village to village, sending the ghost out to cause all sorts of chaos in each one. And in the beginning, he'd loved it. There was a sort of dark pleasure in going about a village in his other form—that of a tiny, unassuming grasshopper—bringing bad luck wherever he went; in souring the milk while it was still in the cows; in emptying the fish traps without leaving a single hole in the weave of the net, so that the fishermen scratched their heads in confusion; in rotting whole fields of crops only on the inside, so that the harvester's hopes lifted at the sight of perfect-looking fruit only for it all to explode in maggots and gloriously bad smells at the lightest touch.

The ghost would look on his work with pride, like an artist admiring his own masterpiece, and chuckle to himself when the villagers came looking for the wise and learned witch, who nodded sagely, took the money they offered her to rid them of their curses, never letting them suspect she was the cause of all their troubles in the first place. Magically, everything would go back to normal, and before long the witch would disappear again, on the road to somewhere new—always before anyone figured out that the true curse had been her presence all along.

But if he was honest with himself, as the years passed, he found it all very tiresome. There was a steady stream of customers at the witch's door, and if they weren't asking for a way to undo her handiwork, they were asking for the same petty meanness, the same tiny bad magics as all the others: a curse on this business, a pox on that house, an impossible-to-remove wart on that one's nose.

Humans, the ghost thought, were just so . . . unimaginative. He was hoping this new master, wherever they might be, would mean a change of pace. New management, as it were.

He pictured the little girl with the pigtails and the wide grin and he stretched out his thoughts, spreading them as wide as he could, listening for the familiar song of the blood calling to him, feeling for its comforting warmth coursing through fresh new veins, pumping through a strong new heart. . . .

He found her in a wooden house on the edge of green, green paddy fields, a house that rattled and shook when the monsoon winds blew.

She was a woman now, tall and tired and pale. Her pigtails had been replaced by a severe bun and her grin had long since vanished, but there was no mistaking that she had the blood. And yet—the ghost sniffed, puzzled—that familiar, calling song was faint and weak, sometimes fading out altogether. And even when her eyes were open, there were shutters behind them that remained very definitely closed. It was as if the light inside her had burned out, and nobody had bothered to replace the bulb.

For a long moment, the ghost paused, wavering uncertainly between staying and going. On the one hand, the witch had been adamant: a pelesit must have a master to control his appetite for destruction, his craving for chaos. Already, he could feel the tug of the darkness, hear the little voice inside him whispering thoughts of ruin and rampage. At the same time, he wasn't even sure this woman's blood would be strong enough to bind him and keep the darkness at bay.

The ghost was still trying to make up his mind when he heard it. The laughter.

This is how he learned that there was also a child.

And the way her blood sang—it was as if she lit up from the inside and made the whole world brighter as she toddled through it, babbling and giggling on chubby bare feet caked with dirt. The witch's song had been rough and raucous, and it swept you up the way a pirate shanty does, or the musical howls of drunkards stumbling home. But the child's song wrapped the ghost in a tender weave of comfort and belonging and glorious wonder, sweet and innocent and intoxicating. And as he watched her, he felt strange new sensations welling up from deep within the cavernous recesses of his chest, a mix of pride and an overwhelming sense that this was a child bound for greatness. What a heady honor to be bound up in it. He hadn't supposed he was capable of such thoughts; the witch had certainly never inspired anything more than prickling annoyance. Was this the change he sought? He needed?

"Suraya," he heard the woman call as he watched. "Suraya. Come inside now. The sun is setting; it will be Maghrib soon." And the little girl scampered unsteadily back to the unsmiling woman and disappeared into the house.

Suraya, the ghost whispered to himself carefully, letting the sound of it play on his tongue like the notes of a favorite song. *Su-ra-ya.* He savored each syllable, marveling at the delicate sounds, at their rhythm and their weight. So this, then, was to be his new master. Not old enough to bind him on her own, nor command him with the words she couldn't quite speak. But he could wait.

When quiet finally descended on the old wooden house, and the night was deep and dark as ink, the ghost wafted into the child's room and stared at her as she slept, hands pillowed under her cheek, her breathing steady and peaceful. There it was again—the sense that he was in the presence of greatness, that he was teetering on the precipice of something bigger than both of them. Carefully, almost reverently, he picked up the girl's plump hand and nipped at her tiny little finger—just a little nip—and drank exactly three drops of the bright red blood that dripped from the cut, sealing it quickly when he was done. Her song was strong and wild, and it almost deafened him as her blood wound through his body, weaving their destinies together line by line, chain by chain. This was more than enough to get by, more than enough to bind them together, until the next full moon hung in the sky.

It is done, he whispered. *And I am bound to you, until the end.*

She shivered slightly under his gaze—she had no blanket— so he curled himself around her for warmth and smiled when she sighed happily in her sleep.

And at that moment, the ghost felt a twinge just where his heart ought to have been, if he had one.

Which he didn't, of course.

TWO

ghost

BY THE TIME Suraya was five years old, she should have broken various bones in her body at least twelve different times, been poisoned twice, and possibly have actually died on seven separate occasions.

Yet she grew like a weed and was just about as welcome as one everywhere she went. It wasn't that the villagers didn't like her; it was just that trouble seemed to cling to her like a shadow or a bad smell. And yet, they muttered to themselves, shaking their heads as she ran helter-skelter past them, she seemed to lead a sort of charmed life: she picked not-quite-ripe fruit from the orchards and never complained of tummy aches; she ran across roads without a single thought for the cars or bicycles that might be zooming past; she climbed trees far too tall for her and fell from them often, yet always seemed to land on her feet; and once, she poked at an ant mound and giggled as angry red fire ants swarmed all over her body, tickling her with their feet and never leaving a single mark. In this way, she went through her days without a care in the world, secure in the knowledge that she would somehow always be safe.

It was harder work than the ghost had ever done in his life, watching and worrying over a young master-to-be who never seemed to think about her own safety and never, ever *stopped moving*. At least three times now, he'd been sorely tempted to cast a binding spell that would keep her arms and legs stuck to her body so that they could both just sit still and catch their breath. But she never stayed in one place long enough for him to even attempt it.

Take today, for instance. He'd already stopped a stray dog from biting her as she'd tried to ruffle its fur, pulled her back from falling into a storm drain, and swatted wasps away from her face as she craned her neck to get a closer look at their nest, all the while clinging precariously to a swaying tree branch.

Once or twice, he caught those dark eyes looking his way and paused, waiting breathlessly to see if she realized he was there—and if she did, if she realized what he was—but she never did. Once or twice more, he'd felt an overpowering urge to show himself to her, if only to tell her to STOP EATING THINGS SHE FOUND LYING ON THE GROUND—but he never did.

The one time they had interacted, it was because she'd spotted him in his grasshopper form in the grass and tried to catch him, giggling gleefully as he leaped his mightiest leaps, heart pounding, trying to escape her sweaty palms and none-too-gentle grip (Suraya loved bugs and animals, but she sometimes loved them *too hard*). He'd thankfully escaped without having to defend himself in some terrifying way, but the close call had been jarring.

One afternoon when Suraya for once wasn't running the ghost ragged chasing her, he sat by her side at the old stone table that stood beneath the frangipani tree in the front garden. Sweat plastered Suraya's hair to her face and neck as she concentrated on a piece of paper before her, her chubby fingers wrapped around a purple crayon, white flowers scattered all around her. The ghost rubbed his spindly grasshopper arms together and wondered idly what she could be drawing that required so much concentration, her tongue poking out of one side of her mouth the way it did whenever she was entirely focused on something. Every few minutes, a blob of snot would creep down from one nostril—she'd caught a cold from splashing through the paddy fields, narrowly avoiding several vicious snakes lurking within the water—and she'd sniff ferociously, sending it shooting back into her nose again.

"Suraya."

The call came from the house, and the ghost watched as her little body immediately tensed, as she always did when she heard THAT voice.

The woman appeared at the door. Little had changed about her in the years since the ghost had first seen her, and she was still a mystery to him. The most he knew was that she was a teacher, which explained her stiff bearing, the chalk dust that clung to her clothing like white shadows, the sharp, acrid smell of the Tiger Balm ointment that she applied liberally to her aching shoulders and back after a long day in the classroom. Every so often, he would put out some feelers and probe her mind, trying to figure her out. But all he found was hints of loneliness and a lot of locked doors.

There were times when keeping them locked seemed difficult for her, though, times when she looked at Suraya with a softness in her eyes, when her hand reached out to caress the girl's hair. Those times the ghost looked at the woman and thought: *There you are.*

Those times didn't come by often, but they happened enough to make the ghost wonder about the woman and the witch and their story, about those letters and the way her handwriting looped and swirled to form that one final terse sentence (*Do not contact us again*). These moments were enough, in fact, to make him feel the merest twinge of sympathy for her. He wasn't sure he liked feeling it; ghosts weren't meant to be sympathetic, of all things.

"Come inside now, Suraya," the woman continued to call, as tall and pale as ever. "It's time for lunch."

"Coming!" The girl snatched her drawing off the table and ran, almost tripping in her eagerness to reach the door. "Look, Mama!" she said proudly, brandishing the crumpled paper. "I made this for you!"

The ghost craned his neck, but couldn't quite manage to see the drawing.

"Very nice," the woman said, and it was as if she was a tube that every last bit of toothpaste had been squeezed out of, leaving her dry and flat. "Now come inside and eat." She paused to glance down at Suraya's feet, which were, as usual, bare. "Mind you wash your feet first, they're filthy." And she turned and walked away, the paper fluttering to the ground in her wake.

Suraya's shoulders sagged, and in their downturned slopes the ghost saw all the sadness and disappointment that weighed so heavily on her young body, and the place where his heart would have been if he had one ached for her.

There had been so many times over the years where he had longed to show himself to her, yet he had always held himself back. The child was still so young, after all. But he yearned to be seen and to be commanded, to be sent out into the world to do her bidding. And if he were honest with himself, he yearned to protect Suraya and her fragile human heart from the cruel, harsh fingers of a world seemingly intent on crushing it to powder.

(This, he told himself, was perfectly natural. A pelesit must have a master, and that master must be protected. Nothing wrong with that.)

"Hurry up, Suraya." The voice held a note of impatience this time.

"Coming!"

As the ghost followed her into the cool recesses of the house, he paused to take in the childish drawing of two purple figures, one tall and one small, holding hands under a bright yellow sun. The tall one had a neat round bun. The small one had a big smile. And in those technicolor scribbles, he saw nothing but loneliness.

It is time, he thought to himself. *It is time she knows who I am.*

That night, while the little girl sprawled on her bedroom floor drawing yet more pictures in the hour before bed, the ghost paced back and forth on the ledge of her open window, trying to calm himself. He did not understand why his throat was dry and tight, or why it felt like his chest cavern was filled with a thousand butterflies frantically fluttering their soft wings, but he wished they would stop. *A pelesit needs a master,* he told himself firmly. *She must know who you are.*

And that was why he slowly unwound himself from his little grasshopper body, rising like smoke, growing and swelling into himself until he stood before her, dark as night and horned and scaled, in all his horrifying glory.

But Suraya merely sat up and looked at him with the same naked curiosity she trained on everything. "Hello," she said, running the back of her hand across her dripping nose and leaving a trail of snot that she quickly wiped on her pink pajama pants.

The ghost paused. He suddenly felt very unsure of himself. *Hello?* His voice came out as a squeak, and he cleared his throat, red-faced. *I mean . . . hello.*

"Who are you?"

He drew himself up and took a breath. This was his moment. *I am a dark spirit,* he announced rather grandly. *I am your inheritance, your grandmother's legacy. I am yours to command. I will smite your enemies. I will . . .*

"What's a 'heritance?" Her big brown eyes were full of questions.

The ghost sagged and sighed. *I'm a . . . present,* he said

finally. *From your granny. She sent me to take care of you.*

"I have a granny?" This time her eyes were wide and full of excitement.

Not anymore, he told her gently, and Suraya slumped. *But you have me now.*

She brightened at this. "That's true," she said, nodding happily. "I have you, and you can be my friend, and we can play together. Only Mama might not like us playing at nighttime, because I'm s'posed to be asleep soon. . . ." The little girl stopped suddenly and clapped a hand over her mouth, eyes wide. "Only I can't tell her about you," she said conspiratorially, leaning close. "She wouldn't like this at all. She doesn't like 'magic and fairy tales and other whimsical nonsense.'" At the last few words she crossed her eyes and put on a mocking, sing-song voice that the ghost supposed was meant to be an imitation of her mother. It was not, he noted, particularly accurate.

I am not a mere playmate, he said disdainfully. *Nor am I a character from some childhood tale. I am a pelesit. I can do whatever you command. And I can protect you.*

"Oooh, does this mean you're like a genie? Or . . . or my FAIRY GODMOTHER?"

I don't grant wishes, the ghost said hurriedly. (*Fairy godmothers! She wouldn't want one of those if she really knew*

18

fairies, he thought, with an indignant sniff. The stories he could tell. . . .)

Suraya's expression moved quickly from eager anticipation to resignation, with a quick stop at disappointment in between. "Oh well," she said with the air of one used to life's many letdowns. "I suppose you can't help that." She paused to scratch the tip of her nose.

"So what's your name?"

My name?

"Duuuuuh." She dragged out the one syllable until it sounded like at least six. "Everyone has a name. See, like this"—she gestured to the rag doll next to her—"This is Nana. And that one's Bingo, and that one's Ariel like the princess, and that one's Saloma like the pretty lady in those boring old movies Mama likes to watch, only I call her Sally because Saloma is just too long, and that one's Suraya the Second because she's going to rule the kingdom after me, and that one's . . ."

The chatter went on, but the ghost barely heard it. Nobody, as far as he could remember, had ever asked him for his name. The witch had only ever addressed him as "you," as in, "You! Go and rot this farmer's entire crop of bananas, would you," or "You! I need you to give this woman nightmares all night so that her competitor wins the beauty pageant."

There was a pause while Suraya took a breath, and he

quickly spoke before she could get going again. *I don't have a name.*

She gasped, looking shocked. "You don't?"

I . . . I don't think so. The ghost felt strangely embarrassed by this and had to remind himself that ghosts don't have feelings.

"That's okay," she said, reaching out a hand to pat him consolingly on one scaly paw. "I'll think of one for you. I'm SUPER good at names. I named all my toys all by myself. And I named that orange cat that likes to come around and steal our fried fish from the kitchen table. He's called Comel now."

Comel?

"Means 'cute,'" she explained seriously, as if he didn't know. "'Cause he's cute." She tilted her head to one side, frowning as she stared at him, her tongue poking out of the side of her mouth, her hand still clutching a bright pink crayon.

The ghost could not help feeling nervous. Names, he knew, existed to give shape to the nebulous, ground the unknown in a comforting reality. He did not think he could cope with being called cute.

Then Suraya brightened. "I KNOW!" she shouted gleefully.

Please don't be Comel, please don't be Comel, please don't be Comel . . .

"Your name is . . . Pink."

PINK?! It was much worse than he had feared.

"Yes!" She climbed up onto her bed and began to bounce up and down. "Pink!"

I am a dark spirit, the ghost said desperately. *I am a powerful being. I have the wisdom of the ages. I cannot be called PINK.*

"But you are! You're Pink!"

He sat down heavily on the tattered carpet and sighed. *But WHY am I Pink?*

"Because." Suraya shot him such a withering look that he felt rather silly for asking. "That's my favorite color." She slipped off the bed and ran up to pat him on the cheek. "You'll get used to it," she told him. "It's a good name. A very good name, maybe the bestest I've made so far."

As good a name as any, I suppose.

Outside, they heard the light, quick step of Suraya's mama. "Quick, hide!" she hissed, and the ghost now known as Pink quickly shrunk back down into his grasshopper form and hopped into the pajama pocket Suraya held open for him, just as the door swung open.

The woman took in Suraya's bright eyes and feverish cheeks and pursed her thin lips. "What games have you been playing in here?"

"Nothing, Mama," Suraya said. "Just drawing."

21

The woman's eyes scanned the room as if she were looking for something, and the ghost felt Suraya's little fingers move protectively over her pocket.

At last, finding nothing, the woman looked at Suraya. "Well then. Time for bed. Go and brush your teeth, and wash your feet or you'll have nightmares. Don't forget to say your duaa."

"Okay, Mama."

The woman swept off back down the hallway toward the living room, where a stack of papers waited to be marked before a flickering television set. And there she stayed for a long, long time, never smiling even as the laugh track played artificial chuckles over the bumbling antics on the screen, her red pen scratching and scribbling busily as Suraya and Pink slept curled up against each other on her narrow bed.

"Tell me about my grandma, Pink."

They were in bed, huddled up together as they always were. It was rainy season once again, and there was a constant, dreary night drizzle tapping on the window. In the darkness, Pink could just make out the outline of Suraya's little head as she leaned against his shoulder.

Again, little one? She asked about the witch constantly; he was running out of stories to tell.

"Please, Pink."

He sighed. *Very well.* He closed his eyes and called up memories of the witch, delicate as smoke wending from a candle flame. *Your grandmother was a small woman, and round, and soft. She had no corners, no sharp edges to her. When she smiled, her whole face crinkled up and her eyes would disappear into two thin lines.*

He did not add that that smile only appeared on her face after she had caused some mischief or other; he often edited these stories in his head before reciting them for Suraya, having long ago decided that there was no point presenting her with yet another disappointing family member. Between her strange, distant mother and her dead father, she had enough of those already.

Suraya smiled. "Tell me the story about the jambu again."

It was her favorite. *There was one day when a little boy was standing just outside your grandmother's garden. Your grandmother had a big jambu tree, so big that some of its branches stretched beyond the fence. And the jambu themselves were miraculous fruits: bright red, crisp, juicy.*

Pink could almost smell the sweet tang of the jambu tree in full bloom.

The little boy was staring up at the tree, his eyes round with hunger. Your grandmother had harvested most of the fruit, but there was one perfect bell-shaped jambu she'd left behind, right near the top—too high for him to reach. *Your grandmother was hanging clothes on the line. She saw him staring up at her tree, and she knew what he wanted. But she herself was too small to reach the fruit, and too old to be climbing trees with her aching back and her quivering knees.*

"So what did she do?" Pink could hear the laughing anticipation in her voice. She knew exactly what would happen next.

She waved her hand, Pink told her. *She waved her hand, and one of the tree branches began to move.*

Suraya giggled, then quickly stifled it before her mother heard. She was meant to be asleep.

Slowly, the branch made its way to that perfect jambu and plucked it with twiggy wooden fingers. Then it passed it to a branch below, which passed it on to the next, and so on and so on, until at last the lowest branch handed the fruit to the little boy, whose mouth hung open in shock and delight. "Thank you," he gasped, looking first at the tree and then at your grandmother. "Thank you." And in answer all she did was put her finger to her lips and wink at him before she went back into her house to get away from the hot afternoon sun.

There was a pause. From down the hall, they could hear the blaring of the television, the old sitcom that was Mama's favorite: "*SO NO ONE TOLD YOU LIFE WAS GONNA BE THIS WAY.*"

Suraya sighed happily. "I always like hearing that story."

I know you do. He never told her what happened afterward as he watched, hidden among the long blades of grass. The little boy bit eagerly into the jambu he had so longed for. There was a yelp of surprise and fear and a heavy, wet *thwack* as the fruit hit the ground, then retching and splashing as the boy turned and vomited into the bushes. The air filled with a foul, sour smell that lingered long after the boy had run off home, tears streaming down his face.

Pink didn't tell her how much work it had been to bend that thick wooden branch, how it had felt to burrow into the hard sweetness of that perfect jambu and turn it into nothing but rot and ruin, maggots squirming through its flesh.

He told himself she didn't need to know. That it didn't matter.

"I'LL BE THERE FOR YOU," sang the TV. *"'CAUSE YOU'RE THERE FOR ME TOO."*

Beside him, Suraya had fallen asleep.

THREE

girl

FOR AS LONG as she could remember, it had been just
the two of them: Mama and Suraya, rattling around together
in the old wooden house that swayed gently in the slightest
breeze. It had taken her a while to figure out that this wasn't
typical; that the families peopling her picture books and the
brightly colored cartoons on TV usually had more than just
two people in them.

"Where's my daddy?" she'd asked her mother once. She
was almost four years old then, still tripping over her words,
fidgeting impatiently while her mother combed the tangles out
of her hair and wrestled the unruly tresses into sedate twin
braids. "Everybody else has a daddy. Mariam's daddy drives
a big truck. Adam's daddy has a 'stache. Kiran's daddy buyed
her a new baby doll with real hair you can brush." Her lower
lip stuck out as she thought sorrowful thoughts about the

injustice of not having someone who could take you for rides in a big truck and buy you toys (she was less sure about the desirability of a 'stache).

She felt Mama's hands still for just a moment, hovering uncertainly near her neck. "He's dead," she said finally. "Your daddy is dead."

"What's dead mean?"

Suraya couldn't see Mama's face, but when she responded, her voice was as dry and sharp as the snapping of an old twig. "It's when people go away and never come back, and you never get to see them again."

Suraya mulled this over quietly, wincing as Mama's nimble fingers pulled at her hair, sending tiny needles of pain shooting into her scalp.

The next day at her preschool, Mrs. Chow, whose stomach had been swelling gently for many months, was not there. The nine little ones under her care, Suraya among them, were told she would be away for a while, and that they would have a different teacher to mind them.

"Yes, Suraya?" Cik Aminah asked, seeing her little hand raised high in the air.

"If she doesn't come back, she's probably dead," Suraya said matter-of-factly.

There had been a call to her home, and a discussion with

her mother. It had not been the first time she had made such unsettling pronouncements in class; it made the other children uncomfortable, the teacher had said politely.

Mama had not been pleased.

By the time she was five years old, Suraya understood that she was different. Nobody ever said it aloud—at least not to her face—but the difference was easy enough to measure. It was in the inches between her and the other kids when they sat on the colorful benches for breaktime snack; in the seconds that dragged by when the teacher told everyone to pick partners, her heart pounding so hard it felt like her whole body shook when nobody reached for her hand; in the twenty extra minutes she waited on her own after everyone else's parents or grandparents or babysitters or maids had picked them up in a riot of cheerful chatter, because her mother had work to finish in the primary school where she taught; in the number of baju kurungs that filled her closet, the matching long tops and bottoms sewn by her mother from the cheap cotton she bought in bulk in the big town, so different from the other girls' colorful skirts and dresses and T-shirts with cartoon characters on them.

Suraya tried her best not to mind this. It was, she told herself, a case of durians. Some people, like her mother, loved the creamy yellow insides of the spiky green fruit with a passion; some people, like Suraya herself, thought it both smelled and tasted like stinky feet. "It's an acquired taste," Mama had shrugged at her as Suraya wrinkled her little nose against the overpowering odor. "You'll learn to like it one day."

Maybe that was what she was. The durian of friends. Maybe people would learn to like her one day. Maybe she just had to meet the right ones.

So until they came around, Suraya kept herself busy. There was plenty to do: the letters in her books were starting to come together, forming delightful stories she could discover over and over again; the scenes and characters she conjured up in her head took shape in technicolor crayon on the pages and pages of old notebook paper Mama brought home for her use; and when she was done with those, there were trees to climb, paddy fields to splash through, bugs to investigate, fruit to pick off trees, and mud pies to make.

So when Pink came along, bursting out of his tiny grasshopper body to show her his true self, she looked at him with the same frank curiosity she looked at everything, and she smiled. When he offered her the seed of friendship, loneliness provided a soil so fertile that she buried it deep in her heart and let it grow and grow until it filled her and patched over the broken bits and made her whole.

"Tell me about my grandma, Mama," Suraya said one evening, while she sat drawing a picture at the kitchen table, picking through markers and trying to choose the perfect colors for her unicorn as Mama made dinner.

She'd been puzzling over this in her head for what felt like ages now, like the mathematics she struggled with in school (Suraya was currently learning to subtract, and was not terribly pleased about it). If she had a grandma once, as Pink had told her, why had Mama never mentioned it? Why were there no stories, no pictures of her anywhere? The only way to find out, she figured, was to ask.

As the words left her lips, she saw her mother and felt Pink in her pocket both go perfectly still at exactly the same time.

"You don't have one," Mama said finally, her back to Suraya, then her knife resumed moving once more, a steady *clack, clack, clack* against the wooden chopping block as she decimated onions and carrots for the daging masak kicap.

Suraya frowned. "That's im-poss-ible," she said. It was a freshly acquired word, and she took a great deal of care in pronouncing it ever so carefully and with a great deal of relish. "Everyone has a grandma. You can't not have a mama."

"I did have one," Mama said. "But not anymore. Not for a long time now."

"Did she die?" Suraya understood death now that she was a whole five years old; she wasn't a baby anymore, not like when she was four.

"Yes."

"But what was she like when she was alive?" Suraya leaned forward eagerly, her drawing forgotten, the uncapped markers drying gently on the table. "What did she look like? What was it like when you were growing up? Did you—"

She had to stop then, because Mama had smacked the knife down on the counter and whirled around to face her, and in that moment she reminded Suraya of the sky right before rain begins to fall on the paddy fields, dark and heavy with a storm of epic proportions. But when Mama spoke, her voice was calm and even, each word slicing through the air like the knife she had just been wielding.

"We do not talk about your grandmother," she said.

And they never did again.

FOUR

girl

WHAT ARE YOU *drawing now?* Pink asked, clambering to the edge of Suraya's notebook to try and take a peek. Suraya was eight now, tall and thin, with skin tanned a ruddy brown from constantly being out in the sun, and a wide, ready smile. Her dark hair obscured the pages of her notebook as she hunched over it on the bed, her pen moving quickly. Suraya never drew with pencil or crayons these days, only black ink.

(*But what if you make mistakes?* Pink would ask, but she only waved him off. "They're never mistakes," she told him. "Only chances to make something new.")

"Shush, Pink," she said now, distractedly. "I'm trying to get this right." She'd been seeing a picture every time she closed her eyes, as though it was seared onto the back of her eyelids, and if she concentrated, she knew she could get it just right on the page.

Pink shrugged. *Suit yourself,* he said, settling into a sunny spot on the windowsill and stretching out his long grasshopper legs so that his entire body could bask in the warmth.

So caught up was Suraya in the movement of her pen, the deft strokes bringing to life an undersea world of swirling waters and the curve of a mermaid's shimmering tail, that it took a while to register the sounds wafting in through her open window. When she finally looked up, she saw in the distance a group of children from the village—boys and girls of about Suraya's age, cycling unsteadily through the trees on hand-me-down bicycles they still hadn't quite grown into. They were children she'd grown up with her entire life—Kiran, with the wide smile and the mass of dark curls; little Ariana, with her short bob and perpetual sniff, the two of them always arm in arm and whispering secrets to each other; Aiman, Ariana's older brother, with his shaggy haircut and an ever-changing map of scars and bruises from his various adventures; David, who once covered himself in glory by chasing a snake off the playground and away from a group of shrieking younger children; and Faris, who had once disastrously tried to hold Suraya's hand while waiting in line for the ice cream man and hadn't really been able to look at her since.

They'd tossed their bicycles aside now and were laughing and shrieking together in a carefree way that made Suraya wince, sending a peculiar pang rocketing through her chest. She saw these kids every day, sat with them in the classroom, knew their names and their families and the scabs on their knees—but when she was around, there was none of this camaraderie, this easy companionship they shared, Kiran's head bent close to Ariana's, David's arm looped easily over Faris's shoulders, Aiman cracking jokes to make all of them giggle. For a moment she imagined herself among them. For a moment she wondered what it felt like to belong.

Pink hopped off the windowsill and sprang onto the bed beside her.

Suraya.

"Hmm?" She barely noticed, still caught up in her daydreams, watching the little group chasing each other through the trees.

Suraya.

"What, Pink?" She glanced at him. "Are you hungry?"

No. You know I do not feel hunger. I am a ghost. I only need your blood for the binding.

"Right," she said. The last binding had been just a couple of weeks ago. It was funny; when they first began, Suraya had imagined a binding would be a magical occurrence that involved colorful sparks and electricity coursing through her veins and a sense that Something Big was happening. In reality, a binding was more like digging out ear boogers: a necessary irritation and a minor discomfort you had to get out of the way every so often so that things worked the way they were supposed to. "Then what is it?" She bent her head back over her sketchbook, trying to shake away the stubborn, lingering aftertaste of heartache.

Listen. Suraya. LISTEN. Why do you never play with the other children?

"What?" She looked up, frowning at him slightly. "What do you mean?"

Well. He scratched behind his antenna with one long leg. *For as long as I've been with you, I've never really seen you play with the other children. It's always just you and me.*

She smiled at him. "You're all I need, Pink," she said. It wasn't quite true, but it was worth it to see the way he held his head higher, pleased and proud. "Besides," she said, turning back to her notebook, "the other kids don't really like me. They think I get away with murder 'cause my mother's the discipline teacher and she'd never punish me, or whatever. And they think I'll tell on them and get them into trouble. And I think they just think I'm weird, and that my drawings are weird." She felt her stomach twist at the thought of her drawings being laid bare for all to see and clutched her notebook close.

Your drawings are not weird. They are beautiful.

She sniffed. "I don't mind. Who needs those kids, anyway?" And in that moment, she meant it.

Pink said nothing, but she knew he was still thinking about it. Pink had a way of playing with his antennae when he was deep in thought, just as she had a way of working her feelings out on the paper. Now, for example, she could tell from the thicker lines, the way she was pressing the pen onto the page, that this was bothering her more than even she would admit to herself. Her art was always truthful, even when she wasn't.

Sighing, she went back to work, her tongue sticking out ever so slightly as she concentrated on the swoops and curves of the mermaid's flowing hair.

Out of the corner of her eye, she saw Pink hop back onto the windowsill and stare out of the window at the little gang outside.

If you were watching him closely, you might have seen his antennae flick forward. Just once. But Suraya didn't.

And then suddenly the laughter turned into screams of terror, and that's when Suraya dropped her pen with a start and quickly leaped out of bed and ran to the window to see what was happening.

The air was so thick with mosquitoes that they blocked out the sun, their shadows throwing the fields into darkness, their collective buzzing so loud it sounded like the combine harvesters that mowed through the paddy fields. They moved in a swarm, quickly and with purpose, bearing down on the shocked children until they were surrounded.

For a moment, the world stopped, as if everyone and everything held their breath, waiting to see what would happen next.

And then the mosquitoes pounced. How they feasted on the children, latching on and supping blood freely from any exposed flesh they could find: arms, legs, faces, necks, ears, all were fair game.

And as the children screamed and screamed and screamed, Pink laughed.

Suraya felt her face freeze into a mask of horror. "Pink." He turned, and in his eyes she saw a dark, wicked glee that made the blood turn ice cold in her veins. "Pink, make it stop."

Fear made her voice quiver, and it was the quiver that dissolved the wickedness in his eyes. He flicked his antennae, and just as suddenly as they appeared, the mosquitoes were gone again, leaving the children bewildered, sobbing, and covered in bright red hives and welts. They scattered, running for their homes, yelling for their mothers, rubbing at the bites that were already starting to itch unbearably.

"Did you . . . did you do that?" Suraya whispered. Her heart was pounding so hard that she could feel her whole body shake.

Slowly, Pink nodded, his eyes never meeting hers.

"What are you?"

Your friend, Pink said softly. *I am your friend.*

Was that true? Was Pink her friend? If he was, why had she never seen this side to him, this darkness, this cruelty? Had he kept it hidden from her? Or—and she felt a whisper of guilt whip around her belly—had it been there all along and she just chose not to see it? She pressed a hand to her temple, as if she could somehow knock all her racing thoughts back into place.

"And why did you hurt those kids?" she said finally.

You are my master, Pink said firmly. *And I am sworn to protect you. And they were hurting you. I would hurt anyone who hurt you. You only have to say the word.*

For just one fleeting moment, Suraya let herself imagine the satisfaction of revenge, of being able to get back at every kid who had ever ignored her, taunted her, pushed her aside. To make them feel exactly how she felt.

Then she thought about the way Kiran's eyes crinkled at the corners when she smiled, and the way Faris's hand had felt when it tentatively brushed against hers, and her mouth went dry. She drew herself up straight and tall and took a deep, steadying breath. "Don't you ever. EVER. Do something like that again." Her hands were clenched into tight fists by her sides, and her eyes were full of tears, but the anger in her voice was great and terrible, and for the first time ever, she saw him shrink back as if to hide from it. "Do you hear me, Pink? Never again. I never want you to hurt anyone, not even for me."

But what if, Pink argued back. *What if you were in danger? What if the only way to save you would be to hurt someone?*

"What kind of danger could I possi—"

What if?

"Fine!" Suraya threw her hands up in the air. "Fine. If I'm in *mortal danger*, if it's the apocalypse, if you need to *save me from the jaws of death*, then you can hurt someone." She couldn't keep the exasperated sneer out of her voice. "But that's it. Do you hear me?"

Pink nodded his grasshopper head, his eyes still trained to the floor, as though he were afraid her anger might burn him.

"Say it. I want to hear you say it."

I will never hurt anyone again, Pink said. *Unless you're in danger. And,* he added quickly, *unless you want me to.*

She set her chin and looked straight at him. "I will never want you to. Not ever."

And that night, for the first time, Pink and Suraya slept side by side instead of entwined with each other, the space between them only inches wide, but big enough to feel like an entire world.

FIVE

ghost

I DON'T UNDERSTAND. *What's the problem?*

They were stretched out side by side on the smooth kitchen tile. It seemed an odd place to lie down, until you realized that it was the coolest part of a house that shimmered and scorched in the afternoon heat.

"The problem," Suraya said quietly, "is that I don't want to go."

But it is a good opportunity for you, is it not? Bigger school. Better teachers. Pink turned over so that the cold tile pressed against his back, and sighed with pleasure. *Is that not what you want?*

"I'm happy where I am." Suraya's dark hair spread around her on the floor like a halo, and her face wore a frown that had appeared the day before, when her mama had made the big announcement.

"Since you've done so well in your exams, I think it's best that you go to school in the big town," she had said, smoothing the folds of her worn baju kurung and avoiding Suraya's eyes, which had grown wide with shock, then dawning horror. "The village school will not be challenging enough for you. I should know, I teach there. And challenges are the best way to grow and learn."

Suraya had said nothing for a long time, appearing to be concentrating hard on moving the rice and fish curry on her plate from one side to the other. When she did speak, her voice was low and quiet. "When do I start?"

"On the first day of school, with everyone else. In two weeks." Her mother got up and busied herself with putting away leftover curry into an airtight plastic container and wiping down the kitchen counters with a damp rag.

"And how will I get there?"

"You'll take the bus in the morning—there's a school bus that will pick you up from the stop just down the road."

"By myself?" Pink heard the uncertain wobble in her voice, and he knew Mama did too, because she clicked her tongue impatiently as she reached up to massage her sore neck. "It's only forty minutes away. That's nothing. You're twelve now, after all, thirteen this year. You're almost a woman, old enough to take care of yourself."

That was the end of the conversation, and Suraya had not stopped frowning since.

"Only forty minutes," Suraya muttered darkly now, splayed on the kitchen floor. "It might as well be light years away. I'll be more of an outcast there than I ever was here."

Maybe the new school might be an opportunity for new friends, Pink suggested. On the ceiling, they were watching two cicaks warily circle each other in a complicated dance, their little lizard eyes darting from each other to a hapless bug crawling in the space between them.

"Considering my track record, I wouldn't bet on it." The smaller cicak darted forward, and before the other realized it, he'd made off with his spoils to a dark corner, leaving the bigger one gaping in his wake.

"I thought for sure the bigger one would get it," Suraya said.

Fortune favors the bold.

There was a silence. "All right," Suraya said. "All right. I get it." She turned her head to look at him. "And you'll be there with me, right? You'll stay with me the whole time?"

A warm glow spread through his chest, and he smiled to himself. Their relationship had shifted the day of the mosquito incident all those years ago; he'd felt her grow wary of him, felt her choose her steps carefully around him, as though he was a bomb that might go off any minute. He'd worried that it

42

would never go back to the way it was. Now it seemed that he was, happily, completely wrong. She still needed him after all.

I am bound to you, he said softly. *Until the end.*

She nodded and shut her eyes.

In the shadows, the cicaks chirped.

SIX

ghost

THE BUS RIDE was long, and Suraya spent most of it sleeping, unused to having to be up before the sun in order to be on a bus by 6:20 a.m. She wasn't the only one, either. In almost every seat, Pink watched as one by one, freshly scrubbed students nodded off, lulled by the bus's gentle rumble. When he tired of staring at their lolling heads or glazed eyes, he looked out of the streaky windowpane instead, as the landscape changed from rolling green to brick buildings, and the world changed from the darkness of early morning to the light of day.

The school was a sprawling old building with graceful arches for windows and an overwhelming air of gentle decay. Pink knew from the fancy brochure Suraya had read aloud to him that this was a premier all-girls school, known for its stellar reputation in academics and athletics, its list of former students a constellation of familiar names and well-known stars. But as far as he could tell, the "premier" label did nothing to hide the peeling paint on the heavy wooden classroom doors; the flickering light bulb in the corridor; the bat poop that clung stubbornly to the red tile floors; the bats themselves, which often took the opportunity to swoop down from the dark recesses of the high ceilings to make the girls squeal; the wooden chairs and tables that wobbled tipsily on uneven legs.

The hall was filled with excited chatter and hordes of girls who seemed to greet each other exclusively in shrieks of joy. The noise set Pink's teeth on edge, but Suraya didn't seem to notice; she'd fished a battered copy of *A Wrinkle in Time* out of her backpack and had settled contentedly in a corner to read, her legs crossed, her back against the wall, the skirt of her turquoise blue pinafore nicely arranged to make sure she wasn't flashing her "coffee shop," as the boys back at her old school had called it.

When Suraya was younger, her mother had sometimes brought home back issues of an ostensibly educational children's magazine the school subscribed to, and one of Suraya's favorite sections had been the Spot the Difference page, her brow furrowed as she concentrated furiously on marking all the ways the two given pictures didn't match: a missing tree branch here, an extra flower petal there. Now Pink played the same game with the scene laid out before him: the deafening squeals of the other girls versus Suraya's silence; the bright, brand-new, freshly ironed uniforms versus the faded softness of Suraya's pinafore and the white shirt she wore under it. Both were hand-me-downs from a neighbor whose daughter had outgrown them; they were fuzzy from use and draped over her thin frame as though it were a hanger instead of a body. He wasn't quite sure why, but the differences made his chest tight and his stomach hollow.

Pink curled into a ball in a particularly cozy nook in the depth of Suraya's shirt pocket and shut his eyes. The school day was long; he might as well take the time to nap.

He was just about to drift off to sleep when he felt Suraya's body tense, like a fist ready to punch.

Suraya?

He poked his head a tiny way out of her shirt pocket to see what was going on. Suraya was still looking down, seemingly focused on her book, and he was about to shrug and slide back into his nook when he realized that her hands trembled slightly, and that they hadn't turned a single page.

Slowly, he looked around her until he spotted them: a cluster of girls, shooting sly looks over at the corner where Suraya sat and whispering to each other.

Whispering about her.

Inside Pink's belly, anger began to spark, warm and bright. They nudged each other and giggled. "Look at her shoes," one stage-whispered, loudly enough for Suraya and Pink to hear, and Suraya shuffled her feet awkwardly, trying to hide as much of them as she could under her too-long skirt. Her school shoes were so old that they were fraying at the seams; the Velcro was fuzzy and barely held together, and there was a hole right above the little toe on her left foot. She'd tried to hide the graying canvas beneath layers and layers of the milky chalk her mother had bought, slathering on more and more with the sponge applicator until the white liquid dripped down her arm and splashed onto the grass. As a result, her shoes were so white they were almost blinding, but also stiff as wood, and as she walked, the chalk cracked, leaving bits of dust in her wake.

On the page of her book, Pink saw one tear fall, then another.

The girls were openly laughing and pointing now, and Pink's anger had grown from a spark to a flame. He had to hold on to his antennae to keep himself from casting a spell he might regret. He'd seen people like this before in his travels: people who needed to step on others to raise themselves up, people who took delight in causing others pain. Many had come to the witch's door seeking out ways to do just that; heck, the witch herself had often indulged in a good old hex or two and laughed long and hard about it. He just hadn't realized they could start so young.

"Maybe that's how they do it in the kampung. Hey, Kampung Girl!"

The shout was aimed at her, but Suraya kept her eyes firmly on her book, refusing to look their way.

"Hey! You, with the torn shoes and that dishrag of a uniform!" More giggles, and this time Pink could see Suraya bite her lip, hard. A single drop of blood pooled beneath her teeth, and she quickly licked it away.

The book was suddenly snatched from her hand. "What could you be reading that's so interesting you can't even reply when someone calls you, Kampung Girl?" This girl was clearly the leader, her long straight hair tied back in a high ponytail with white ribbon, her uniform still crisp and clearly new. Her shoes were white canvas, but designed to look like ballet slippers instead of the plain old Velcro or lace-up sneakers the others had. A shiny gold *K* dangled from a chain on her bright pink backpack.

"I didn't know you were calling me," Suraya said finally, her voice calm and even. "That's not my name, after all."

"Your name is whatever I choose to call you." Pink heard a

thunk as the book was tossed to the floor. "It could be Kampung Girl. It could be Smelly. It could be whatever I want. Understand?"

Suraya said nothing, and K's eyes narrowed. "I said. Do. You. Understand."

One of the girl's minions, a pretty girl with dark skin and a mass of long curls, tugged on Suraya's long braid once, hard, so hard that it made her yelp and brought tears to her eyes. But Suraya nodded very slightly—at least enough to satisfy K.

"Very good." The girl leaned in close, and Pink smelled bubblegum-scented shampoo and baby lotion. "You don't belong here," she whispered. "And I'm not going to let you forget it."

The bell rang then, signaling the start of assembly, and the girls scattered to line up with their classes, leaving Suraya breathless, scrambling to get up and gather her things, her eyes still glassy with unshed tears.

As she walked quickly to her line, she left a trail of white dust behind her.

Thankfully, K and her minions weren't in Suraya's class, and Pink could feel her body relax as she slipped into the familiar routine of a school day: new books, new teachers, new things to learn. Suraya's mind was a sponge, and she never seemed to mind what was put in it so long as there were interesting things to soak up and absorb along the way.

The bell for recess sounded, and Suraya made her way to the canteen, gripping a plastic container she'd hastily filled that morning with a banana, a boiled egg that her mother had received at a wedding and left on the kitchen table, and three bahulu from the heavy glass jar on the kitchen counter. The banana was riper than she'd thought, and she had to peel it carefully so that it wouldn't fall apart; even so, when she took a bite, she somehow managed to spill a huge chunk of banana mush down the front of her pinafore. It looked like she'd been sick.

From a table nearby came a chorus of familiar giggles, and Pink turned to see K and her gaggle of girls looking at Suraya and laughing. He turned back, his face contorted in his most ferocious grasshopper scowl. He could tell Suraya was trying not to cry as she dabbed at the stain furiously with a tissue. *Eat the bahulu,* he told her gently. *You'll feel better.*

She shook her head slightly at him.

Suraya. Eat.

This time she obeyed, though not without a small sigh. The round, seashell-shaped little sponge cakes had always been her favorites, but now all she could do was turn it around and around in her hands, nibbling at the edges. As she did, Pink saw her steal a glance at K's table, and at K's brilliant turquoise lunch box, adorned with stickers of the latest K-pop boy band sensation. When she opened it, they could also see that each of the lunch box's sections was filled with food: a heap of fried noodles, still steaming slightly; a slice of yellow butter cake; a handful of cookies studded with chocolate chunks; picture-perfect orange slices, plump and juicy. "Oh look!" K's face somehow managed to look both pleasantly surprised and unbearably smug. "My mother is *so* thoughtful. Isn't it nice when someone cares enough about you to pack you a *proper* lunch?"

That, Pink decided, was quite enough. If he had to sit here one more minute and watch Suraya's cheeks burn and her eyes water, he might actually scream.

Instead, he flicked his antennae.

K's table was in the middle of laughing raucously at yet another one of her not-that-funny jokes when one of them happened to look down at her own lunch box.

The screams echoed to the rafters and shook the bats awake from their slumber as girls jumped up and tried to get as far as they could from the table, their faces pale. Some were retching; K made a great show of heaving dramatically over the closest dustbin.

Suraya stood up, bewildered, trying to see what was going on. And then she saw, and blinked, and looked again.

Because if you weren't concentrating, you could have sworn that the food in those abandoned lunch boxes was moving.

Except then you looked closer and you realized the terrible truth: that every lunch box on the table was so full of worms and maggots that if you stayed quiet enough, you could hear the sticky squelch of them writhing and wriggling through noodles and fried rice and porridge and cake and whatever else those unsuspecting mothers had so lovingly put in them this morning.

Suraya pushed her own container with its meager lunch way, way back onto the table.

Then she walked quickly away from the shrieking girls and the chaos, past the frangipani trees that bloomed beside the cafeteria, slipping carefully into the narrow passage between the row of classrooms and an old building that was mostly used to store broken furniture and assorted bits that the school administration wanted to get out of the way. Back here, there was one more frangipani tree all on its own, light filtering through its spreading boughs and dotting the ground with puddles of sunshine, and this is where Suraya stopped. There was nobody else here; it was as if nobody even knew it existed.

Pink felt her hand slide carefully into her pocket, and he

jumped onto it so she could draw him up into the light. In the place where his heart would have been there was a hammering and a pounding that rattled his tiny body and made him jumpy. Would she be grateful? Would she understand that he did things only for her protection?

Instead, she was frowning, and the pounding inside him turned into a strange sinking feeling.

"Why did you do that, Pink?"

They were harming you. He tried to maintain a defiant pose, sticking up his little grasshopper chin, but to do so to his master felt like insolence. *I did only what they deserved.*

"But I never asked you to. Didn't I tell you that before? Not to hurt anyone unless I ask you to?"

Well. Um. Suraya's eyes never left his face, and Pink began to feel horribly hot and squirmy. *Yes,* he admitted finally and—it must be said—reluctantly. *Yes, I believe I recall you saying something like that, now that you mention it.*

"And did I ask you to hurt those girls?"

Not in so many words.

"I didn't, Pink."

He sighed. *Fine. You did not ask.*

"So you disobeyed me. Never again. Do you hear me?"

In the distance, he could hear the steady murmur of chattering girls as they clustered together, waiting for the bell to ring. *I hear you,* he said sullenly. *But why? Why not give them the same pain they give you? Measure for measure. An eye for an eye.*

"I don't want anybody's eye."

You know what I mean.

Suraya was silent for a while as she thought about this. Then she sighed. "Because then, that makes me no better than them. That makes me a bully too."

The bell rang and she quickly slid him back into her pocket. Just before she began running toward her class, she glanced down at him and smiled—a weak and watery smile, but a smile nonetheless. "Thanks," she whispered.

Pink felt pleasantly warm all over. *You're welcome.*

"But don't ever do that again."

SEVEN

girl

THE DAYS PASSED, as they always did. Suraya survived them as best she could, working hard at her classes, avoiding K—whose name, as it turned out, was actually Kamelia—and the rest of her gang of bullies when she could, tolerating their torments when she had to.

Thankfully, their paths didn't cross often—Kamelia was fourteen and in form two, a whole year ahead—but they were grouped into the same sports house. Twice a week, after classes, Suraya had to change into her track bottoms and bright red house T-shirt with a gnawing pain in the pit of her stomach and the miserable knowledge that Kamelia and her goons would find new and creative ways to make her life difficult when they could. Often, she would get home and catalogue the fresh bruises blooming all over her thin body, the result of spiteful pinches, well-timed pushes, and once, a hard kick to the shin when nobody was looking.

Pink watched grimly through it all. *I could hurt them, you know*, he told her. *I could shatter each of their bones into tiny pieces. Make them sorry they ever even looked at you. Make them pay. It's what the witch would have done.*

It appalled her that his dark streak reared its ugly head so easily these days. But she just shook her head. "No, Pink," she said. "For one thing, I am not my grandmother. And for another . . . well, they'll get tired of it eventually. And besides, better they do it to me than some other girl who might not be able to handle it."

She saw him peer more closely at her face and tried her best to rearrange her drooping mouth into a smile. *But you cannot handle it, actually,* he said.

Suraya felt her mouth pinch tight together. Pink had a way of saying things that made her feel the exact opposite of how he wanted her to feel when he said them, kind of the way her mother telling her not to sing so loudly around the house made her want to scream every line to every song she knew until the rafters shook. Pink was the extra parent she'd never asked for. She could tell he wanted her to break down, agree with him, admit that he was right, and all she wanted to do right now was cross her arms, dig in her heels, and prove him wrong. "Silly Pink. Of course I can."

She knew that he knew she was lying.

This is when the odd things began to happen.

They weren't happening to her, which is why at first, Suraya didn't really notice them, in the way that you don't really notice a single ant meandering lazily along the contours of your foot. But when one ant becomes two, and then seven, and then seventeen, and then a hundred, the pricking of their tiny feet and the stinging bites of their tiny teeth become harder and harder to ignore.

This is the way it was. It began with nothing, really: one day, there was a stone in one of Kamelia's pristine white canvas shoes that made her limp and curse, and which wouldn't dislodge itself no matter how many times she shook the offending shoe. On another day, her geography workbook was drenched and soaking, even though she'd fished it out of a perfectly dry backpack. On yet another, the marker exploded in her hand as she worked out a math problem on the whiteboard, covering her from head to toe in black ink.

On and on and on it went, and at first, it was easy enough to brush off as a mere run of terrible luck. Only, the bad things kept on happening, and somehow they only ever happened after Suraya had been the victim of one of Kamelia's cruel jokes, and soon this link became impossible to ignore.

Coincidences, Suraya thought desperately to herself, trying hard to ignore the memory of Pink's flicking antennae, the wicked grin on his little grasshopper face. But the day they played volleyball during PE and Kamelia somehow managed to get hit by the ball nine times in a row—once as a hard smack to the shoulder, which made her squeal so loudly it echoed through the courtyard—even Suraya had to admit that coincidences could only explain away so much. Kamelia's gang didn't know what was going on, but they did know that somehow, whenever they did something to Suraya, something happened to them in turn. And they didn't like it.

I should talk to Pink, Suraya told herself firmly. *Ask him what's going on. Tell him to stop, if he's the one doing all of this.* But she never did. Sometimes she told herself that it was because she was certain he would stop by himself; sometimes she told herself it was because it wouldn't make any difference anyway. What she never told herself was the truth, which is that she didn't want to start a fight with her only friend in the entire world.

She didn't want to go back to being alone.

Waiting for the bus home one afternoon, a shadow fell across the whirling dragon Suraya was sketching in her notebook. She tried her best to ignore it, tried to focus on the scales she was painstakingly and precisely inking on its great tail, but her trembling hands made the pen hard to control.

"What have you got there, Kampung Girl?"

Around her, the other girls waiting for the bus, sensing trouble, quickly walked away.

"It's nothing," Suraya said, quickly snapping her book shut and fumbling with the zipper of her backpack, trying her best to stuff it inside before they could get it.

Too late. Divya had snatched it right out of her hands and was riffling through the pages with her long fingers, nails shaped to delicate points. Divya was Kamelia's best friend, and she took particular delight in digging those nails hard into Suraya's arm when teachers weren't looking, so hard that they left deep red half-moons in her flesh for days afterward, so hard that Suraya often had to bite her lip to keep from yelping.

Divya was grinning now, her eyebrows arched, her eyes wide in exaggerated mock-surprise. "Look at this, K," she said, tossing the book to her friend. "She thinks she's some kind of artist."

Kamelia flipped through the little book, frowning. "Wow, Kampung Girl. Looks like you spent a lot of time on these. You must really like to draw, huh?"

Suraya stayed mute, her eyes never leaving the book in Kamelia's hands. She had learned early on not to trust the older girl's seemingly pleasant tone or inane conversation. Her words were like a still river; crocodiles floated just beneath the surface, ready to catch you with their sharp, sharp teeth.

"It'd be a shame if . . . whoops." A sick ripping sound tore through the afternoon air, and Suraya stifled a gasp of horror. "Oh dear. However did I manage to do that?"

Divya snickered. "Here, let me take that before you do any more damage . . . uh-oh." Another tear, so harsh it seemed to pierce right through her heart. Divya stared right at Suraya as she crumpled the paper into a little ball, smiling a nasty smile. She tossed it over her shoulder into the open drain behind her; as it sailed gracefully through the air, Suraya caught a glimpse of ornate dragon scales.

"We're just so-o-o clumsy," she said, and Kamelia laughed.

"Stop," Suraya whispered. "Please stop." But all this did was make them rip faster and laugh harder, and soon nothing was left of the notebook but its thin brown cover, bits of paper dangling pathetically from its worn spine.

"Don't worry," Kamelia said soothingly. "We'll get rid of this trash for you." And they tossed it into the deep, dark drain and ran off home.

Suraya walked slowly over to the drain's edge and watched for a long time as the stinking water carried the little white pieces away, like pale ships on a filthy sea. She never even wiped away the tears that coursed silently down her cheeks.

EIGHT

ghost

IT WAS THE demise of the notebook that sent Pink over
the edge.

He'd spent the rest of the day trying his best to make Suraya
smile. He'd gathered her favorite flowers—wild jasmine—and
sprinkled them all over so that her whole room was filled with
their sweet scent. He'd enticed the bees into giving him some
of their fresh, golden honey, which he collected in a cup made
from leaves—Suraya loved honey and lemon in her tea in the
evenings. He'd even slipped away as she did her homework to
go to her old school, creep into the teachers' lounge where her
mother sat marking papers that afternoon, and whisper a suggestion in her ear. That evening, Mama came home bearing
piping hot packets of Suraya's favorite nasi lemak from the stall
near the post office, the coconut rice, sambal, hard-boiled egg,
and fried chicken all still steaming as they sat down for dinner.

It might have worked. It might have made Suraya's heart just a little lighter. But for Pink, it wasn't nearly enough.

That night, he sat on the windowsill staring out into the inky blackness as Suraya slept. He did not move for a long, long time.

When he finally did, it was to rub his long back legs together. The familiar chirp of the grasshopper's song echoed out into the darkness. If you were listening, you might have dismissed it as just another part of the soundtrack of midnight, along with the buzzing of the mosquitoes and the chirping of the geckos. But then again, this song wasn't meant for you.

Then, there was a tiny skittering sound that grew louder, as if hundreds of little feet were running, then they stopped right beneath Pink's window. He bent his head low and whispered his instructions. It took a long time.

Eventually the little feet skittered away again into the shadows, and Pink curled up with Suraya as he usually did, a satisfied look on his face.

The next day, Kamelia and Divya weren't at school. And when they did return, days later, they sported new identical short haircuts and sullen expressions.

"Why did they do that?" Pink heard Suraya whisper to a classmate. "I thought they loved their hair."

"They did," the classmate whispered back. "But my mom was at the pharmacy the other day and she met Divya's mom and Divya's mom told her that they had the most TERRIBLE lice infections. Like, so bad that it looked like their hair was MOVING, all by itself. Divya's mom just, like, had no idea what to do."

Suraya touched her own long hair, in its neat braid. Pink knew she loved her hair and couldn't imagine cutting it all off. "Couldn't they just have used some medicine? Did they really have to cut it?"

"It was so bad the medicine wasn't even working anymore! They both had to get their hair cut, and I heard they CRIED." This was said with a particular relish; everybody in the lower school feared the two girls, and they certainly didn't mind them suffering, at least a little bit.

"Poor things," Suraya said softly, and the other girl snorted.

"If you say so," she said. Then she quickly slipped away. It wouldn't do to be seen talking to Suraya, not when the new girl was so clearly in Kamelia's crosshairs.

Pink poked his head out of Suraya's worn shirt pocket to drink in the sight of the two girls, their long, shiny hair now cropped close to their heads, and smiled a slow, wicked smile.

It was only what they deserved.

NINE

ghost

AFTER THE LICE incident, Kamelia and Divya's reign of terror seemed to lose steam. They didn't exactly stop being their mean, bullying selves, but they seemed to shrink slightly, as if losing their hair meant losing some of their power.

For Suraya, this meant happier, lighter times. She could often make it through entire school days with nothing worse happening to her than a tug of her braid or a small shove in the chaos before assembly. It didn't mean making friends became any easier—unpopularity is a leech that's hard to shake off once it sinks its teeth into you—but she accepted this as she always had, and was content. She put her head down in class and concentrated on her work; she spent every recess with Pink in the secret spot they'd found on the first day of school, in the dappled sunshine that filtered through the frangipani leaves. Slowly, Pink could feel her unclenching, settling in, settling down, and he was glad.

In fact, Suraya and Pink could quite happily have gone on this way forever, if not for the new girl.

She appeared one day about a month into the school year, standing quietly next to their teacher Puan Rosnah as she made the introductions. "Class!" Puan Rosnah clapped her plump hands hard, and the sharp cracks brought an abrupt stop to their chatter. "Class! We have a new student. Her name is Jing Wei, and I'm sure you'll make her feel very welcome." There was an obvious emphasis on the last two words, and the class snickered. Suraya looked with interest at this new girl, who was gazing back at her new classmates in a way that seemed entirely unconcerned. She was small, this Jing Wei, with black-rimmed glasses that seemed to take up half of her face, a sunburned nose, and hair cropped short like a boy's—a rare sight in this school, where hair served as a sort of status symbol, and the longer and shinier it was, the better.

Introductions over, Jing Wei slipped into a seat in the middle of the class and took out her history book. If she was aware of the curious stares and hushed whispers of the other girls, she didn't show it.

It was pouring with rain when the bell rang for recess, and the girls raced for the best spots in the canteen and the school hall. Suraya followed slowly, her hands clutching her plastic lunch container, her eyes on the new girl. Jing Wei walked serenely among the boisterous crowd, carefully staking out a spot for herself in a stairwell just off the hall, away from the noise and the damp. She had a book in one hand and her own lunch box in the other.

Pink could feel Suraya hesitate. *Go and talk to her,* he said. *Go on. Why not? We've got nothing to lose.*

(Later, Pink would think back and wonder why he'd said this; why he hadn't just said *Come, let's go sit over in that corner, just you and me, like we always do.* But big moments don't come with price tags, and Pink would have no idea how much this moment cost him until much later.)

Her chest heaved as she took a deep breath, and Pink almost lost his balance in her swaying pocket.

"Okay," she muttered under her breath. "Okay. Let's do this."

She walked over and stood awkwardly in front of the new girl, who looked up from her book. "Hullo," Jing Wei said cheerily. "I'm Jing Wei, who're you?"

"I'm Suraya." She shuffled her feet. "Is it okay if I sit with you?"

"Ya, of course." Jing Wei slid over to make room for her on the step, and Suraya sat down, smiling shyly. "I got pork in my lunch though. Is that okay?"

"Ya, it's okay, I don't mind."

"I know some Malay girls don't like when I eat pork near them." Jing Wei shrugged, spooning another heap of rice into her mouth. "But I dunno why. Not like I force you to eat it also, right?"

"Right." Suraya took a small bite of the kaya and butter sandwich she'd made for herself that morning and glanced down at the other girl's book. "What are you reading?"

Jing Wei's small face lit up. When she smiled, her eyes crinkled up until they almost disappeared. "It's a great book! It's called *A Wrinkle in Time*. You know it?"

"Know it! I've read it like four times!" Suraya's smile was so wide it nearly cracked her face in two. "It's one of my favorite books."

"Wah, four times! It's only my first time, but I'm almost halfway through already. I like that Charles Wallace, he's damn smart."

Suraya nodded, wiping a spot of kaya from the side of her mouth. "You like to read?"

"Oh ya." Jing Wei scraped the last of her rice out of her container, which was black and shaped like Darth Vader's helmet. "My mother said that's how I ruined my eyes, because I read all the time. As if that's a bad thing. You read a lot too?"

"Yes. I . . . don't have many friends, so I have a lot of time to read."

"Hah? No friends? Why ah?" Jing Wei regarded her with frank curiosity, pushing her glasses back up her nose, and Suraya shrugged.

"I don't know," she said. "I'm new to this school, and I live pretty far away. But even back home I don't have many friends. I guess other girls just . . . don't like me."

"You seem okay to me." Her smile was wide and friendly. "And you like to read too! If you like Star Wars then we're definitely going to be friends."

"I've never seen Star Wars," Suraya confessed, and then began to laugh at Jing Wei's expression of open-mouthed dismay.

"Ohmygoooooood, never seen Star Wars? You serious? You have to come to my house and watch it, I've got all of them, on Blu-Ray somemore."

It was the first time Suraya'd ever been invited back to someone's home, and Pink thought his nonexistent heart might burst with happiness and pride.

"Okay," Suraya said happily. "Okay, I will. And you can come to my house and look at my books."

"Cool!"

"Hey, are you done?" Pink frowned; Suraya's own container was still half full of the soggy sandwiches she'd put together that morning.

"Ya, why?" Bits of rice flew out as Jing replied through her last mouthful.

"I want to show you this secret spot I like to go to during recess, before the bell rings. You know. To get away from people."

Their secret place? Pink felt his heart sink. Their own special spot, the one place they went to for a little peace during the chaos of the school day?

She was taking this strange new girl to their secret place?

Pink felt it then: a shimmer in the air, a ripple that told him change was coming, a hot flame of anger licking delicately at his insides. We have nothing to lose, he'd told Suraya, but suddenly he wondered: She *has nothing to lose. Do I?*

But Suraya and Jing Wei noticed nothing. They raced happily toward the frangipani trees, secure in the knowledge that they'd each found a friend.

TEN

girl

SURAYA HAD WATCHED the animated movie *Pinocchio*
exactly once, and then never again, because the bearded pup-
pet master Stromboli, with his dark beard and his wild eyes,
freaked her out and gave her nightmares for a week. She'd
taken the DVD and hidden it in the crack between the book-
case and the wall, where there was space for little else but dust
and geckos. It was, as far as she knew, still there.

But when she looked back on the moment she met Jing Wei,
she would say that, much like the little boy made of wood,
this was the moment that she felt like she became real. This
was the moment she began to blossom into herself. It was as if
having Jing accept her showed her that it was okay to accept
herself too. She stopped stooping and trying to hide behind her
hair; she walked tall and looked people in the eye when they

spoke to her. And it was refreshing to have a friendship she didn't need to hide, for once.

With Jing Wei by her side, she learned to laugh, and even to make jokes of her own. They were never apart, and the other girls got used to seeing the two of them together, the tall, lanky figure of Suraya beside the petite Jing, who barely came up to Suraya's shoulder. The two exchanged books, shared their food—as long as it was halal, of course—and talked about everything, from what they'd read to their families. Suraya even showed Jing her notebook, a new one, its thin blue lines slowly filling with a cast of colorful characters, improbable scenes, fantastic beasts. She'd held her breath as Jing flipped slowly through the pages, and didn't let go until she heard Jing's breathless, drawn-out "Cooooooooooooooooool."

Jing had a huge family, a cast of thousands, and her stories were often peopled with colorful characters: grandparents, uncles, aunts, and a never-ending stream of cousins, whom she divided into cousin-brothers and cousin-sisters.

She was fascinated by the idea of a family consisting of just two people. "But you don't have any cousins or anything?"

"No," Suraya said. "It's just me and my mother."

"And your dad?"

Suraya looked down, studying the frayed tips of her shoes intently. "He died a long time ago. I was really little. I don't even remember him. My mother never talks about him."

She looked up to see Jing looking at her with frank sympathy and understanding. "It's okay. My dad died too, you know." She pushed her glasses back up from where they'd slid down her nose. "Just last year. He loved Star Wars. We used to watch all the movies together, have lightsaber battles." She lapsed into silence, and Suraya's heart ached for her.

"How did he die?" she asked gently.

"Heart attack. He didn't even know there was anything wrong. He had a pain, he said. We thought resting would help. Next morning . . ." Her voice trailed off, and Suraya thought she detected a glint of tears behind those glasses. "Anyway. That's why Ma moved us back here, so we could be closer to family."

Suraya nodded. "I wish we had more family," she said wistfully.

Jing glanced at her. "You have me now what." Her tone was light, but her hand brushed against Suraya's as she spoke, and her smile lit up her entire face.

"I do," Suraya said. Her answering smile was so wide it made her cheeks ache.

She went on the first of many visits to Jing Wei's house, a neat, modern affair in a neat, modern neighborhood ten minutes from school. Jing's mother—"Call me Aunty Soo, dear"—picked them up in her car, a trim red Mercedes-Benz, and served them fried rice she'd bought from a stall nearby for lunch. "Halal, darling, don't worry," she'd said, patting Suraya's shoulder with a perfectly manicured hand, the nails painted bright red. "I purposely went to buy from that stall because I knew you were coming. Ha, eat, eat, don't be shy ya, you want somemore you just ask."

"Okay, aunty," Suraya said, her mouth full, her heart so happy she thought it might burst.

Jing's room was big and sunny, like her personality, and full and colorful, like her life. The walls were painted a soft blue, and there was an entire wall of shelves crammed full of books and DVDs and toys. "I used to play with those when I was small," she said quickly as she saw Suraya's eyes linger on the worn dolls and teddies. "Not anymore." There was a desk with a shiny laptop and piles of books and notebooks, and in the corner, Jing's own small TV and DVD player.

Suraya ran her hands along the books, craning her neck to read their spines while Jing Wei popped a DVD out of a case on her desk and crammed it into the player. "Come on, come on!" she said, grabbing Suraya's hand and forcing her to sit down on the bed. "Okay," she said, standing next to the

TV with the remote in her hand, a serious look on her face. "There are prequels, and there's the original trilogy. I'm gonna make you watch the original trilogy first, 'cause the prequels suuuuuuck."

"Does that mean I don't have to watch them?"

Jing stared at her, wrinkling her nose. "Of COURSE you have to watch them, Sooz. I just mean you watch these ones first, because then you'll get why people love these movies so much. Then only you watch the others so you get the full story. Understand?"

Suraya smiled and rolled her eyes. "Okay, cikgu. Teach me the way of Star Wars."

They watched them all as the weeks passed, in between doing their homework and talking and eating the snacks that Jing's mother pressed on them in between, from fresh pisang goreng, the batter fried to crispy golden perfection, the banana inside still warm and steaming, to ais krim potong, blocks hand-cut from frozen ice cream, skewered with sticks, and flavored with everything from mangos to lychees and deliciously refreshing on hot afternoons. The more she was there, the more she experienced of Jing's seemingly charmed life, the less willing Suraya was to let Jing see her own. Jing almost forgave Suraya for never quite being as excited about Star Wars as she was, though that didn't mean she stopped trying to stoke her enthusiasm for it. But she never understood why Suraya wouldn't invite her to her house.

"I could go with you on the bus what," she said. "And I could see your room and your books, and you could show me the orchards and the paddy fields. I've never even *seen* paddy fields in real life, Sooz." Jing Wei had spent her whole life in cities and towns; Suraya's stories of climbing trees and plucking fruit right from the branch fascinated her.

Suraya thought of Mama, distant and cold, and the shabby wooden house on the edge of the paddy fields. The idea of Jing setting foot into her bare little room was enough to make her shudder. "No lah," she demurred, trying to sound casual. "It's too far, and my mom is always working. Better I come here."

"Then can't I come on a weekend, or something?" Jing pressed on. "Some time when your mom isn't working. She can't be working all the time lah right?"

"Right," Suraya said. "I'll ask her."

She never did. She was quite happy with her life as it was, quite happy to endure Kamelia and Divya, and the long bus ride later in the day that brought her home close to sundown, if this warmth and friendship was what she got in return. And eventually, Jing stopped asking.

Mama, for her part, never asked where she'd been all day;

she just assumed, Suraya guessed, that it was a school thing.

She realized that being Pink's friend was like dancing on the edge of a precipice; it was fun, and you were on solid ground as long as you didn't slip, but you worried about that line separating you from the darkness *all the time*. Being friends with Jing, by contrast, was like . . . just dancing, with a partner who matched your every move. It was easy and free, balancing and satisfying. It felt right. It felt *good*.

And so life went on, in a way that made Suraya the happiest she had ever been.

ELEVEN

ghost

BUT WHAT ABOUT Pink?

This was a question that Pink found himself asking constantly as Suraya watched movies and ate meals and spent hours talking and giggling with Jing. *What about me? What about me, Suraya, what about me?*

No longer did they spend their time idling in the sunshine, or lying on the cold kitchen floor to escape the heat, or nestled in the crook of tree branches, Suraya's feet swinging in the air as they talked. She turned to him less and less as he lay curled up in the pocket of her school shirt, listening to the rhythm and music of her day. She often dozed off on the long bus ride back home from Jing's house, leaving Pink to stare out of the window as streaks of orange and rose wove themselves through the darkening sky, and at home, between dinner and bed, there was barely any time to talk at all. "G'night, Pink," she'd say sleepily as they curled up together the way they had for years, but even as she slept peacefully in his arms, Pink could feel that he was losing her. They were bound together by blood, as they always were—but she'd never been so far from him.

Do you not think you are spending too much time with this girl? he'd asked her one day, trying to mask his anxiety, the fretful note that crept into his voice.

"No, I don't think so," she'd answered, with a puzzled smile. "At least, I haven't heard her complain about it. Why?"

It doesn't leave much time for other people. By *for other people*, Pink really meant *for me.* But he was hoping she'd understand that on her own; it felt vaguely embarrassing to have to talk about his emotions like this.

"There's really nobody else I'd want to spend that time with anyway," Suraya had said, and the way she laughed as she said the words, so careless, so lighthearted, tore right through his chest.

And he didn't know what to do about it. What was this feeling, this sense of loss? Loneliness? Fear? Resentment? The ghost didn't know. All he knew was he didn't like it, not one bit. Ghosts, he told himself sternly, were not meant to feel things. Therefore, he couldn't possibly be feeling those things, yes? Yes.

The only way he knew how to cope with this mysterious new sea of emotions he found himself navigating was by hanging on to the one thing he did recognize: anger.

Anger was good. Anger was familiar. Anger was nourishment to a dark spirit like himself. He could *work* with anger.

But how?

The source of his anger, Pink knew, was Jing Wei. Jing Wei, with her smug little grin and her irritating giggles and her whispered confidences. Jing Wei, who had waltzed into school with her offer of friendship and stolen his Suraya away, the way the witch used to lure children with those perfect, mouth-watering jambu.

And so it was to Jing Wei that he directed his anger.

His magics were small at first. A lost storybook, one of her favorites. A scratch on her favorite Star Wars DVD (*The Empire Strikes Back*, a movie far superior, she insisted to Suraya, than all the others), rendering it unplayable. A smack to the face during a game of netball, shattering her glasses into three pieces and bruising her cheek. An ink blot blossoming on the pages of her English essay, eating up the neatly written words until only a third could be seen, earning her a sharp rap on the knuckles from Miss Low's heavy wooden ruler— Miss Low never could tolerate any carelessness in homework. A hole in the pocket of her pinafore, so that her pocket money worked its way out and she had to go without the new Millennium Falcon figurine she'd been saving up for. "I don't know how it happened," she told Suraya, blinking back tears of disappointment as they frantically retraced her steps. "It's never happened before."

It was never anything that couldn't be blamed on bad luck or carelessness, never anything big enough like the last time, for Suraya to glance suspiciously at Pink and his antennae.

Or so he thought.

It was a perfect Saturday afternoon, the kind with blue skies dotted with fluffy white clouds, the kind sunny enough to bathe everything in a warm glow, but breezy enough to make venturing outside for more than five minutes actually doable.

Are you not spending today with . . . your friend? Pink asked as Suraya made her bed, her hair still damp from the shower. He couldn't bring himself to say her name.

"Not today, Pink," she said, smoothing the sheets down neatly, folding her blanket into a perfect rectangle. "I thought it could just be you and me today."

Just you and me? He felt light suddenly, as though someone had lifted an invisible stone from his back.

"Like old times." Suraya smiled down at him, and he smiled back, nodding.

All right then, he said. *What shall we do?*

"What we always do," she said, grabbing her sketchbook and clipping her favorite pen to the loop that held it shut. "Head to the river."

The river was a small one, just barely big enough to avoid being called a stream, and its appearance was governed by its moods. Sometimes it was calm and flowed at a sedate pace between its grassy banks; sometimes it grew swollen with the rains and flowed fast and furious, sweeping up everything that crossed its path and swallowing it whole.

But there was no danger where Suraya and Pink sat, on a rocky overhang that jutted out a little over the water, perfectly shaded by the trees overhead. Sunlight streamed through the leaves and dappled the water in pretty patterns of light and shadow. Suraya sat cross-legged and bent over her sketchbook, her pen flying busily over the page, and Pink curled up in a warm patch and dreamily watched the dragonflies play over the water. That's how he would have been content to stay all day, until Suraya opened her mouth to speak.

"Pink."

Hmm? He looked over at her, still feeling warm and altogether too comfortable; he was about to fall asleep.

"I want to talk to you about something." She set her pen down now and looked right at him. The page was covered in trees; a pathway leading into a forest, the branches closely woven so no light could get through, each leaf meticulously inked into place.

Oh? He sat up then, shaking himself awake. *What about?*

"It's about Jing."

Pink's ears prickled at the mention of her name. Even the sound of it was enough to set off tiny sparks of anger in his chest. *Oh?* She sounded serious, and for a moment he thought she might say she didn't want to be friends with Jing Wei anymore, and he felt almost giddy with delight at the idea.

There was a long pause before she continued, as though she was trying to find the exact right words. "I know what you've been doing to her, Pink."

He frowned. *I don't know what you mean.*

"Yes, you do." She looked steadily at him, holding his gaze until he had to turn away from her big brown eyes. "You do, Pink. You know exactly what I'm talking about."

He fiddled with a blade of grass, not saying anything, not meeting her eyes.

"You have to stop, Pink. She's my friend and you have to stop."

I used to be your friend, he said sullenly. *Your only friend.* He knew that last bit was nasty, but he couldn't stop himself.

"I know. And you are still my friend. But Jing is too, and

what you're doing isn't nice." She sat back and sighed, sweeping her hair off her neck and tying it into a messy ponytail. "I tried to let it slide, those first few times. But losing the money—that made her so sad. She was really looking forward to buying that figurine, you know. She's been saving forever."

Pink said nothing, crossing his grasshopper arms tight.

"Will you stop?"

If she expected an answer, she certainly wasn't getting one. She sighed again. "Come on, Pink. Don't make me do it."

Still he refused to answer, or even look at her.

"Fine," she said, standing up and brushing the dirt from the bottom of her jeans. "Fine. You forced me into it." She towered over him, her eyes glinting with anger, and he couldn't help shrinking slightly. "I am your master," she told him, her voice hard and cold. "And I command you to stop playing your tricks on Jing Wei. Do you understand?"

There was no disobeying her when she used that tone, and Pink nodded. "I understand," he muttered.

"Good. Then that's settled." She picked up her sketchbook and turned to go. "Come on. I'm getting hungry."

Pink hopped along slowly in the grass behind her, and with every minute that passed, his anger grew and grew until he thought he might burst in a brilliant explosion of fire and rage.

Jing was a poison, a virus that had worked herself into

Suraya's life and taken root. It was only his duty, he told himself, to cut her out before she did any real damage. No matter what he'd told Suraya. No matter what he promised.

A pelesit protects his master. And that girl would get her due. He would see to that.

TWELVE

ghost

PLOTTING HIS REVENGE was, in the end, the easy part. Pink had plenty of time to lay down his plans, plenty of time to think and scheme as he rocked and swayed in the pocket of Suraya's school uniform. The hard part was figuring out how to make sure Suraya wouldn't find out. But even that, in the end, wasn't that hard. Between school and Jing Wei and her books and her sketches, there was plenty in her life to keep her happy and occupied. She was content. She was also distracted, which made his plan easier even as it sickened him. She didn't even think about Pink or what he was doing. And he needed to put a stop to it. He needed her to go back to needing him—almost as much as he needed her, though that last bit he refused to admit even to himself.

In the end, it was the bullies that were the key.

He'd promised to leave Jing alone, after all, and a pelesit

would never disobey his master. But there was a way. There was always a way.

And it was simple enough. Simple to have red paint fall just so on the seat of Kamelia's chair, so that she sat on it unawares.

Simple enough to use a little notice-me spell as he clung onto her ballet slipper shoes, something that made everyone turn to look at her as she walked to the canteen from her classroom, the last one in the farthest block. Simple enough to make sure everyone noticed the bright red stain on her pinafore, looking for all the world like fresh blood blooming freely into the turquoise cotton, every girl's nightmare.

Kamelia was usually the one whispering and giggling at others behind their backs—and to their faces, for that matter—so suddenly finding herself on the other side of things must be incredibly unpleasant, Pink surmised from the way she quickened her pace, the way her hands clenched and unclenched themselves as she walked. She quickly found Divya in the canteen and gripped her arm. "What is going on?" Pink heard her hiss as he clambered quietly up the rough weave of her white socks to get a better view. "Why is everyone looking at me like that? Do I have a pimple or something?"

Divya scanned her face, frowning. "No lah, where got? I don't see . . . oh my god!" She clapped her hands to her mouth, and Kamelia's eyes widened.

"What? What? What's going on?"

"Come with me to the toilet. Right now." She steered Kamelia over to the nearest bathroom, walking behind her to try to shield her from the amused gazes of the others and shoving the two girls who happened to be washing their hands at the sink roughly outside before locking the door.

Minutes later, there was an agonized shriek from behind the closed door.

Pink smiled. In just a few moments, the two girls would come storming out, red-faced and raging, determined to find out who had committed this dirty deed, and who would they find with red paint on their hands? Who else but Jing Wei, who had been charged with the task of decorating the classroom for Chinese New Year, which just happened to be that month; Jing Wei, who had come early to school to finish painting an enormous cloth banner with red firecrackers and the words HAPPY CHINESE NEW YEAR; Jing Wei, who had chosen the exact shade of red paint that currently adorned Kamelia's skirt.

It was simple. So simple.

All Pink had to do was sit back and wait for his revenge to be complete.

THIRTEEN

girl

IT WAS SURAYA who found her in the end, at the bottom of the stairs farthest from the hall, whimpering, blood trailing from her nose. Her right arm stuck out from her body at an angle so unnatural that Suraya had to look away. By her knee were the shards of her black-rimmed glasses. Someone had stomped on them hard, grinding the lenses into powder.

She knelt down quickly, bending over Jing, her eyes wide with concern. "Jing. You okay?" It was a stupid question, she knew it even as the words were spilling out of her mouth. But what else could you say in the face of such obvious pain?

"I can't move my arm, Sooz," Jing whispered. "Everything hurts."

Suraya touched her friend's face gently, pushing back the hair that fell into her eyes. "Don't worry," she whispered back. "I'll go get help, okay? I'll be back as quickly as I can."

Then she ran off down the corridor, yelling for a teacher with a strength and volume she never knew she was capable of.

They took Jing Wei away in an ambulance, the sirens blaring, the red and blue lights casting weird shadows on the beige school walls.

The official story was that she fell down the stairs.

But as Suraya was ushered away by the school nurse, who gave her a cold, sweet chocolate drink to sip and made her lie down in the sick room "for the shock," she saw serious-faced officials take Divya and Kamelia into the principal's office across the way and shut the door, both girls pale and frightened and curiously deflated. Just as they passed, Divya had grabbed Suraya's hand. "We didn't mean to do it," she'd whispered hoarsely, her palm sweaty, her voice laced with anxiety and regret. "It just happened. It was an accident." Later, peeking out of the sick room window, she saw their parents. Kamelia's mother was dainty and fair, and wore high heels and a haughty expression; Divya's mother was plump and worried-looking, her hair streaked with gray and making its way out of the loose bun she wore low on her head.

Suraya lay there for what seemed like hours on the lumpy mattress in the sick room's single bed and thought about faces: Jing's sweaty face, contorted in pain; Kamelia's face and

Divya's too, looking more scared than she'd ever seen them; Pink's face and its wicked grin upon seeing hordes of mosquitoes descend on playing children. Each face came with a different emotion: first worry, then anger, then frustration, then fear. With every passing minute each emotion grew bigger and more tangled up with another, until she thought she might burst from trying to contain so many feelings.

When the school day was finally over, just before they boarded the bus, Suraya took Pink out of her pocket and brought him up close to her face, so that he got a good look at her hard eyes, her flared nostrils, her gritted teeth. Her grip was suffocating.

"We will talk when we get home," she told him, dropping each word like a stone.

Then she put him back in her pocket and they rode the bus in silence, all the way back to the little wooden house by the paddy fields.

FOURTEEN

girl

THERE WAS A familiar tall thin figure waiting for them when they got off the bus, and Suraya blinked in surprise. Her mother had never met her at the bus stop like this before.

"Hello, Mama," she said, then paused, unsure of what to say next.

"Hello." Mama's pale face was illuminated by the glow of the setting sun, which was busy setting the sky on fire as it plunged below the horizon. "Your school called. They told me about your . . . friend."

"Oh." Suraya looked down, thinking of Jing's pale face, her blood-spattered uniform.

"She will be fine." And Mama reached out a hand and patted Suraya stiffly on the shoulder, twice.

Jing's mother might have gathered her up in a hug, she

thought, held her close, let the warmth seep into her tired, heavy limbs, kissed her aching head. But Suraya knew that this was the best she could hope for, and she appreciated the gesture for what it was.

"Yes," she said, with a confidence she didn't feel. "She will, I'm sure."

"Well then." Mama turned and began to walk toward the house. "Come on," she said over her shoulder. "I made gulai lemak ikan and sambal belacan today. You need a bath before you eat, you have blood on you."

Suraya looked down, confused. There were blood stains on her knees, and another running along the length of her fore-arm. She hadn't even noticed.

Her stomach growled and she realized that, despite every-thing, she was hungry.

Slowly, she followed her mother into the house.

In the darkness, Suraya searched for the right words.

She had been looking for them for a long time. Through her shower, staring at the water as it dripped down the pale blue tiles into the drain at her feet. Through dinner, where the silence was punctuated only by the sounds of mealtime: chew-ing, water sipped from glasses, the clink and scrape of metal against ceramic as Suraya and Mama scooped food onto their plates. Through prayers as she went through the motions, bending and bowing.

Until now.

Suraya was in bed. The only light in the room came from the crack under the door, and from the weak moonlight that straggled in through the window.

And then, finally, she spoke.

"Pink."

Yes?

A pause. "Why did you do it?"

He paused, as though thinking about this. *I do not know,* he said finally. *I do not like the girl, and I wanted to see her hurt.*

"Why don't you like her?"

I do not know, he answered. *I just do not.*

"You do know." Her voice was quiet. "Tell me why you don't like Jing, Pink."

It was a long time before he could speak again. *Because you like her,* he said sullenly. *I do not like her because you like her.*

"I do like her. She's my best friend, the first real friend I've ever had. She's the reason I've finally been HAPPY. For the first time in my whole life."

The watery moonlight caught his little grasshopper eyes, and in the darkness they seemed to flash. *And me? Have we not been happy together, you and I? What have I been to you, then, all this time?*

"I don't know," she answered honestly. "You're just . . . you. You can't be the kind of friend Jing is, Pink." It was hard to get the words out.

And so what kind of friend must I be?

"The kind that doesn't hurt my other friends, for one thing."

There was a long silence. Suraya stared out of the window at the lights in the distance and prayed for the strength to say what she knew she must.

"I've been thinking, Pink."

The nerves almost choked her, making it hard to get the words out. Suraya paused, and it was as if the whole world paused, waiting for the words that would change everything. When they finally came, they came in a rush, as if they were relieved to finally escape her tongue.

"I think it's time you stopped following me around."

There was a hiss, like air escaping a balloon. But Pink said nothing.

"I'm twelve now, almost thirteen. I'm making my own

friends. I have my own life. I don't need you tagging along and destroying things whenever you feel like it."

I am bound to you, Pink said then, his voice barely above a whisper. *I am bound to you, until the end.*

"Then this is the end, Pink."

The words were hard to get out.

You dare dismiss me? Just like that? After all I have done for you?

"Done for me?" She felt a spark of rage. "So you're saying I should be grateful?"

I have done nothing but protect you. I have done nothing but be your friend. He paused. *For a long time, your* only *friend.* The slight, sneering emphasis was faint, but it was there, and Suraya heard it.

"And I never asked for that protection! I never asked for any of this! You took my blood without my consent, and now you think I should bow down and throw myself at your feet? You never gave me a choice!" She threw off the covers and sat up in her bed, glaring at him. "I am your master, and I command you to leave."

Then I will, he snapped. *I will. But you will find you cannot be rid of me so easily.*

And with a sound like thunder, he disappeared.

Suraya leaned back on her pillows, exhausted. Her heart

pounded hard in her chest, a steady rhythm that echoed in her head and made it ache. But despite all of this, what she felt most was relief. Pink, she thought hopefully, would soon come to see that this was best for both of them.

In the meantime, for the first time in a long while, she would face the world tomorrow without her ghost on her shoulder. And there was so much of it to explore.

FIFTEEN

ghost

HOW DARE SHE? HOW DARE SHE?

He had done nothing but watch over her. Protect her. Be her companion, her guide, her family.

Love her.

And this was how she repaid him?

To leave him—banish him—for a mere human girl?

He would show her.

He would show them both.

SIXTEEN

THE FIRST DAY without Pink, Suraya woke up feeling as light as a cloud. She floated through her usual morning routine: brush your teeth, make sure to get that little gap between those two front ones, good job Suraya, now shower, oops, that water's cold, dry yourself carefully everywhere, every little bit, that's it. It was strange to think that the only voice occupying her head was hers. She felt giddy and effervescent, her thoughts fizzing like bubbles floating to the top of a glass of ice-cold cola. And she carried that feeling with her all day long, and into the next day, and the next. Pink was a good friend, she could admit this to herself unreservedly, but being friends with him was like walking a tightrope. You had to be careful where you stepped, what your next move would be. You had to be watchful and wary and alert always. You could never relax.

And so even though Jing was in the hospital, even though

Suraya worried about her friend, even though she spent most of her time alone, even though she felt a tiny pang of guilt about feeling the way she did . . . she was also, in a way, happy. She sat with Jing for hours, playing card games, trading her stories of teachers and fellow students and school-day woes with Jing's stories of doctors and nurses and patients and their visitors. She filled page after page of her sketchbook, pictures leaping from her pen as if a dam had been removed from its tip. She read for hours, sitting in a pool of sun on the rocks by the river and trying not to think about the last time she was there, with Pink, and the harsh words they'd exchanged then. In fact, she tried not to think about Pink at all.

Of course, like it or not, she was going to have to start thinking about him again very soon.

The problem with parting ways with a friend, particularly when that friend happens to be a supernatural being, is that they often take out their displeasure at your decision in ways that go far beyond the realm of human possibility.

The first sign of Pink's rage was the smell.

It appeared a few days after the breakup. Suraya woke up from strange, disturbing dreams that she couldn't quite remember, only to be greeted by a horrible stench, a stench like bad eggs and rotting corpses, a stench so bad she thought she might actually throw up.

She jumped out of bed and flew out of the door to find her mother. "Mama," she called, holding her nose. "What is that terrible smell?"

But her mother just looked at her strangely from where she stood, slicing carrots for soup. "What smell?"

Suraya stared, open-mouthed. "What do you mean, what smell? This smell, the one like . . . like . . . like the garbage truck on a hot day!"

Still Mama just looked at her, and Suraya soon realized that nobody else smelled the smell but her—not Mama, not any of her classmates or teachers, not Jing or Jing's mother when she visited them at the hospital, not a single person but Suraya herself.

It was Pink, she knew, Pink punishing her for what he thought of as her disloyalty, Pink expecting her to call on him, apologize, beg to be saved.

But if that's what Pink expected, he didn't know her at all. Suraya gritted her teeth and endured the smell. Days went by, and still she endured. She endured it as it coated her tongue and rendered food inedible; she endured it as it made water turn sour in her mouth; she endured it as it blanketed her in a layer of filth that made showers futile. At night, when she finally fell asleep, it crept into her dreams and tinged them with darkness.

The nightmares were the second sign.

She came home from school one day to find her mother in the kitchen, stirring a pot on the stove. "Set the table," Mama said, ladling steaming curry into a big white bowl, and so she did, pulling glasses out of the cupboard above the sink where they were kept, setting the big blue plates carefully in the center of the yellow placemats. Mama put rice on her plate, a big helping of thick curry lumpy with contents that Suraya couldn't quite make out. Together they read the pre-meal duaa, and then Suraya tucked in, making a neat parcel out of the rice and curry and fresh greens and sambal with her fingers and shoveling it into her mouth. It was delicious, though she couldn't quite make out what it was, and with every mouthful she tried to figure it out. Was it fish? Chicken? Beef, perhaps? Each time, the answer eluded her.

Finally, she turned to her mother. "What is this in the curry, Mama?"

"Ladies' fingers," her mother replied, chewing placidly.

Suraya frowned. "But that can't be it," she said, poking the morsels on her plate, which looked nothing like the long green pods her mother often added to curries or fried in sambal. "This tastes like meat. Not vegetables."

Mama stared at her as though she'd said the stupidest thing in the world. "No," she said again. "They're ladies' fingers." And she picked up the bowl and shoved it into Suraya's face so that the curry was inches away from her nose, so that she could see for herself the fingers swimming in the thick brown gravy, some long and thin, some short and squat, some still wearing their nails, others with bare spots where nails ought to be. "It was quite challenging harvesting enough," Mama said nonchalantly as Suraya choked and spluttered. "But I managed it, in the end. All you need is a good sharp knife. . . ."

Suraya never heard the rest because she started to scream, and it was the sound of her own screams ringing in her ears that woke her up with a start, cold sweat streaming down her face.

That was only the first. There were more, many more, sometimes two or three on the same night. She often mused, during the daytime when the world was flooded with light, that the dreams would have been fine if they were merely peopled with strange creatures and horrific monsters. Those she could handle. The problem was that the nightmares were twisted versions of reality, vivid scenarios that started out perfectly normal and quickly spiraled out of control, and so real that she sometimes had trouble figuring out what had really happened, and what hadn't.

By the time Jing Wei came back to school, it had been two weeks since the red paint incident and the rainy season was in full swing, each day an endless gray blur of drizzle and dreariness. Suraya saw her as she stepped out of her mother's red Mercedes, carefully shielding her cast from the rain as she made her way into the hall, and her heart lifted crazily. "Jing!" she called, waving wildly. "Over here!"

In the distance, she could see Jing's face light up as she ran over. But the closer she got, Suraya thought she saw her face change. And when they hugged, it was Jing who held her gently, as if it were Suraya who was broken and not the other way around.

"What's the matter?" Jing said, the first words out of her mouth.

"Matter?" Suraya frowned, confused. "Nothing's the matter. I missed you so much!"

"I missed you too." Jing's grin was wide, but there was a hint of worry playing on the edges. "But are you sure you're all right? You don't look like yourself."

Suraya shrugged. "Just been having some trouble sleeping," she said. It was, of course, a bold-faced lie. Between the smell and the nightmares, she'd barely eaten or slept in the past two weeks, and she knew that it showed—more than once, teachers had pulled her up sharply in class for not paying attention, and the world was starting to take on a hazy, unreal quality, as if she were wandering through a fog all the time.

Still, Jing was back, and with her friend beside her, Suraya felt like she could handle anything Pink threw her way.

So she linked her arm through Jing's and smiled. "I have so much to tell you," she said. "Wait till you hear—Mrs. Sumathi has a boyfriend!"

"No way!" Jing's eyes were wide, and she drew closer to hear this tantalizing gossip about their English teacher, who wore ornate sarees and a perpetual frown. "But she's ancient, though!"

"Way! And her boyfriend's, like, ten years younger than she is! Jane's mother saw them together at the cinema . . ."

And as they walked arm in arm through the sea of girls waiting for the bell to ring, you might have heard a low growl in the shadows, felt it ripple through the air. Or you might have thought it was thunder ripping through the rain. Who knows? Suraya was just happy to have her friend back, and she didn't hear a thing.

SEVENTEEN

ghost

SOMETIMES HE FELT bad. Sometimes he thought twice, three times, four times, five, about flicking his little antennae and turning his once-beloved master's life to chaos.

Not his master. Not anymore. Just Suraya. Just some girl.

I am a dark spirit, he told himself firmly. *Created to perform dark deeds. She cut me loose, and now she must pay the price.*

It was easy. He just let all his anger and his jealousy and his hurt and his pain lead the way.

And the entire time, he tried to ignore the twinge in the pit of his stomach that just didn't seem to want to go away.

EIGHTEEN

girl

ONCE, AT JING'S house, they'd been watching a movie—
not Star Wars, for once. It was meant to be a romance, one of
those will-they-won't-they setups that you know are actually
a they-will-because-they're-the-two-best-looking-people-on-
the-screen types. Jing, surprisingly, was a sucker for sappy
movies. Only this one kept stuttering and skipping, until Jing
popped it out of the DVD player and buffed it vigorously with
her sleeve.

The next phase of Pink's haunting made Suraya's life jump
like a scratched-up DVD. Swathes of time would pass in the
space of a blink, without her even realizing it.

Skip.

There they were at the table, Mama and Suraya, and Suraya
was silently rearranging the rice and sambal jawa and freshly

fried fish into shifting patterns on her plate, trying to make it look like she was eating.

Skip.

She opened her eyes to find herself in the shower, gasping and spluttering under the furious spray, lungs desperate for air, the skin on her fingers and toes wrinkled to the consistency of raisins. *How long have I been standing here?*

Skip.

And now she was in her bedroom, sitting at her plain wooden desk, her sketchbook open before her, pen in hand. There was a picture on the page in front of her: an intricate tangle of flowers and leaves and vines in stark black ink on the snowy paper. *Did I draw that?* She must have, somehow, only . . . only she couldn't quite remember.

She stared at the page and sighed.

Something on the page sighed back.

Suraya's heart began to pound hard in her chest, a rhythmic thudding that echoed in her ears.

Beneath the flowers, somewhere in the dark spaces where the vines and the leaves intertwined, something began to move.

She could see it, dark and writhing, and she could hear it, its breath a wet, heavy rasping, and she could feel it, most of all—an icy coldness in the tropical heat of her bedroom, a hole ripped in the canvas of reality. Its movements were slow and sinuous, and she couldn't shake the feeling that it was coming closer to the surface, ready to break free of its paper prison.

The movement stopped, and it was like the entire world held its breath.

Then slowly, softly, ink began to bleed in thin little lines down the page, from the very center of her drawing down, down, down to the bottom of the page. From there, it moved in steady streams and rivulets across the desk, pooling in the dings and scratches on the surface on its way to the edge. And then finally, it began to drip steadily onto the floor at Suraya's feet.

And though she trembled like a leaf in a storm, she stayed where she was, first because she was so afraid, and later because she couldn't move if she wanted to. The ink that puddled on the floor grabbed at her feet, tiny strings of black reaching up to latch onto her skin, weaving a net to keep her where she was. Then as she watched, it slowly began to creep up her legs, turning everything it touched black as midnight, steadily laying claim on her body as if it was its own to take.

Just as she felt the slick touch of it on her neck, she heard a voice whisper in her ear, a voice that sounded remarkably like Pink's.

You will not be rid of me so easily.

NINETEEN

girl

THEY DIDN'T TALK about that night ever again. Not about how Mama had burst into the room, her face a mixture of shock and confusion at the sound of Suraya's piercing screams. Not about how she'd had to pry her daughter's stiff fingers from where they clutched the edge of the desk so hard that the nails had gouged dents into the wood; Suraya had had to pull out three splinters afterward, each long thin sliver piercing through her skin like a tiny spear. Not about how the sobs had stopped only so that Suraya could empty the contents of her stomach—not that there'd been much in there to begin with—down the front of Mama's batik kaftan.

Instead, Mama went into teacher mode, full of talk about Actionable Next Steps. "You are clearly not well," she said, after cleaning them both up and popping Suraya into her bed.

"We will see a doctor tomorrow."

She patted her daughter's pale cheek hesitantly, as if she'd studied it in one of the books she taught her students. "You will be okay," she said.

"Yes, Mama," Suraya murmured sleepily, exhausted from wrestling with vomit and nightmares. Did doctors treat ghostly maladies? It was worth a shot, she supposed.

The doctor's room was hot and humid, the only air coming from a lone standing fan that whirred noisily as it rotated from left to right and back again. "Sorry ah, air cond rosak," the plump nurse murmured as she showed them in, pointing to an aging air-conditioning unit that looked as if it had been there since air conditioners were invented. Suraya's skin prickled in the heat, and as she pushed the long sleeves of her baju kurung top up to her elbows, she wondered how much sweat was trapped under the nurse's black hijab. As the nurse walked away, the cloth covering her head writhed and moved, revealing not hair beneath, but a wriggling mass of dark snakes gasping for air. One hissed at Suraya primly—*What're you looking at?*—before tugging the hijab back into place with a fanged mouth.

Dr. Leong was a pleasant-faced older man, his dark hair

streaked with gray, his glasses thick and rimmed in tortoise-shell. He tutted as he looked Suraya over, placing his cold stethoscope on her chest to listen to her heartbeat, sticking a thermometer in her ear to check her temperature. "Temperature okay," he said to Mama, who sat clutching her purse on her lap. "No fever. But she looks quite skinny for her height, and she's very pale. You eating, girl?" He poked her gently in the ribs, smiling a toothy smile. "Not doing one of those diet things you young girls like so much, right? Boys don't like girls too skinny, you know."

Good thing I don't particularly like boys who have stupid opinions about my body, Suraya thought to herself. She knew his type. So many adults ask you questions without any real interest in listening to your answers, and Dr. Leong was one of them.

So she just smiled weakly at the doctor and focused on the posters on his wall: a faded food chart. What You Need to Know about Shingles. A bright yellow poster with a harsh crimson line slashed across a sinister-looking mosquito, bearing the slogan Destroy Aedes, Defeat Denggue. She tried not to let the misspelling bother her, and failed.

The mosquito turned its head to look at her. *He'll destroy you,* it whispered. Suraya shivered.

"Watch her diet," Dr. Leong was saying to her mother. "Maybe some supplements. She needs more iron." As expected, he spoke as if she wasn't even there.

Mama was nodding and gathering herself up to leave when he coughed delicately.

"It also looks like she got some things on her mind," the doctor said, with the air of a man who realizes he's tiptoeing through a field of thorns. "Maybe you want to take her to a therapist? Some counseling? I know not everyone believes in that kind of thing . . ."

Mama's face was like a window with its curtains tightly drawn. "Thank you, Doctor," she said, rising and gesturing for Suraya to do the same. "We will certainly take all your suggestions onboard."

"Sure, sure." He drew a neatly folded handkerchief out of his pocket and mopped his forehead with it; Suraya had not known there was a man left on the planet who still carried a handkerchief. As she watched, the white square flopped forward slightly at the corner, revealing an open, yawning mouth that began to gnaw at the doctor's face. "Just a suggestion, you know."

"Of course."

He coughed again, this time with a note of apology. "Pay

bill outside, ya." He slipped the handkerchief back into his shirt pocket and waved them goodbye, and Suraya tried to ignore the gaping wound that bloomed on his cheek, painfully red and oozing blood. *It's not real,* she told herself. *It's not real, it's not real, it's not real.*

As they walked to the car, Mama with her purse, Suraya with the white plastic bag that held pills she knew would do her absolutely no good at all in one hand and a small piece of paper excusing her from school for a few days ("So you can get some rest," Dr. Leong had said) in the other, she found her voice. "I don't need a therapist," she told Mama. It surprised her how timid she sounded.

"We'll see," was all Mama said in response.

They got into the car. The afternoon heat had turned the seats into searing hot flesh roasters, and Suraya was careful to keep her hands away from the burning leather.

They baked gently all the way back home.

Time oozed by slowly that day, and the day after, and the day after that. Mama went to work as usual, though not without a long list of instructions for Suraya. "Rest well. Don't forget to eat. And take your medicine like a good girl." There were no hugs or kisses; but then again, there rarely were.

The heat, the smell, and the constant struggle to maintain her grip on reality made Suraya's head ache. Still she battled grimly against her visions, turning her head when the shadows the trees outside threw on the wall melded together into something that grinned menacingly at her, gritting her teeth when Mama presented her with a plate of staring eyeballs where meatballs should have been, ignoring the flesh that melted off the faces on the TV show they watched after dinner, leaving only the perfect teeth of the actors gleaming in their clean white skulls.

He can't go on like this forever, she thought to herself. *He loves me. Pink loves me.* But with each fresh horror, she believed it a little less.

Drawing helped. She spent many an afternoon at her desk, bathed in sunlight, hunched as usual over her sketchbook. Opening it—touching it, even—had been a struggle after her nightmare, but she told herself she was being silly. It was a dream. Dreams weren't real.

Her pen flew busily over the book, comfortably familiar in the crook of her hand. She was working on a study of hands—she never could get hands right, they were such tricky things—and the page was filled with them: hands with fingers spread apart; hands clenched into tight fists, each knuckle carefully shaded; hands with long, elegant fingers; hands with stubby fingers and nails caked in dirt; hands reaching out as though asking for help.

It was a relief to think about something other than Pink, for once.

She leaned back with a sigh, rubbing her aching back, satisfied with the work she'd produced. The last hand was the best one so far, she thought, the play of light and shadow perfectly rendered, the position of the fingers poised, natural. "Good job," she told herself aloud.

On the page, the fingers twitched.

She did her best not to notice. "All done," she said quickly, slamming the book shut. "Why am I even talking to myself?" she muttered.

But she knew it wasn't herself she was talking to.

The sketchbook moved on her desk, very slightly.

She stared at it. It looked unassuming enough, its familiar black cover scratched and slightly dented from use.

As she watched, it moved again, shifting ever so slightly closer to the edge of the desk.

She got up then, walking quickly to the window. Outside, the sun shone almost unbearably bright on the village, bleaching everything white and making her eyes water. "Nothing is happening," she whispered. "Everything is fine. Nothing is happening. Everything is fine." If she said it often enough, it might come true.

There was a bang, so loud that it made her whirl around, her heart pounding in her throat.

The sketchbook was on the floor, open to the page filled with hands. And the hands were moving.

Not just moving; they were reaching up and out of the book, pushing past the paper barrier, beckoning her closer.

Suraya ran.

She leaped over the book, feeling the phantom hands just graze her right foot as she flew over them, and ran straight for the door, banging it shut behind her, leaning all her weight against it as she breathed hard, palms clammy, heart still banging in her chest like a drum solo.

From behind the door, there was silence.

And then there wasn't.

It was a strange sound, a sort of rhythmic thump and scrape that she couldn't quite work out. Slowly, she kneeled on the floor and bent down to peer through the sliver of space beneath the door.

The hands were making their way closer and closer, gripping the floor for purchase and dragging her sketchbook along inch by inch behind them.

She leaped up and backed away. There was no way for them

to open the door, surely? Her thoughts swung wildly first one way, then the other. Should she scream? Should she run?

And then suddenly, she felt a wave of anger wash over her.

She was tired of running.

And she was tired of this.

"Come and get me, you jerks!" she yelled.

The thumping stopped.

Then one by one, she saw them burst out from beneath the door: a dozen paper-white hands straining to reach her. The air was filled with agonized, angry shrieks, a hundred high-pitched voices raised in fury and frustration. Suraya put her fingers over her ears, trying to block out the sound, but there was no escaping it.

Her eyes fell on where the iron stood on its board in the corridor, between Mama's room and her own, just so they could each get to it whenever they needed to without disturbing the other. It was black and old-fashioned, so heavy that lifting it made her arms ache.

She could use it now.

With the shrieks and screams ringing in her ears, Suraya grabbed the iron and brought it down with all her strength on the outstretched hands trying their best to swipe at her ankles, mashing them into the floor. And then she did it again. Then again. She didn't stop until all that was left was a mess of paper and ink puddling on the floor like blood.

The final scream was long and terrible and filled with so much rage that it made her tremble.

When it finally died away, when nothing was left but silence, she let the iron slip from her quivering fingers with a clang and slithered to the ground, her knees suddenly too weak to hold her weight.

"I can't do this anymore, Pink," she said, and her voice was sad and broken. "I can't keep going on like this. You have to stop doing this to me."

But this time there was no reply, not even from the mosquitoes that buzzed around her.

girl

THEY'D HAD A talk about bullies at Suraya's old school once. It was run by one of those passionate young teachers who descended upon the village starry-eyed and with big plans in their heads and left a year or two later crumpled and weary and drained. The type who spoke in ALL CAPS when they were excited about something.

"Bullies are just INSECURE, and taking their INSECURI-TIES out on YOU," the teacher had said, practically glowing with enthusiasm (only two months into her stint, the stars still shone bright in her eyes). "You must STAND UP to them. And if that doesn't work, you MUST tell an ADULT so that they can HELP you." Her voice dripped with sincerity. "You DON'T have to face this ALONE." Then they'd run through some deeply embarrassing role-playing exercises where nobody had been quite as invested as the teacher had hoped.

Suraya wasn't sure how much of a difference that teacher had made. But she figured that she'd had a point about telling an adult. After all, when you have a problem at school, you raise your hand and someone comes to help you. And this was the biggest problem she'd ever faced in her life.

It was time to raise her hand.

It was the hour between dinner and bedtime, and Mama was sitting at the dining table, piles of exercise books towering in front of her. Her red pen worked its way busily down page after page, the scratch of its nib against paper punctuated only by the disapproving click of her tongue when she came across a particularly silly mistake. For once, the nightmares kept their distance; the pen stayed a pen, the books stayed books.

Fortune favors the bold, Pink's voice whispered in her ear, and she almost wanted to laugh at how strange it was to think of him now, of all times.

Instead she took a deep breath and walked up to the table.

"Mama?"

"Hmm?" Mama looked up, deep lines of irritation scrunching up her forehead. The fluorescent light caught the threads of silver running through her black hair and made them glow. "What is it?"

"I have . . . a problem."

"Hmm." Her mother closed the book she was marking with a soft thump and peered at her, and Suraya felt her stomach shrink. "What kind of problem? Is it maths? Your teacher used to tell me you never concentrated properly in maths. Maybe you need extra classes."

"Umm, no, that's not it." The absolute last thing she wanted to add to her ever-growing list of reasons her life currently sucked was more maths. "It's more like . . . a problem with bullies."

"Bullies?" She had Mama's full attention now, and she wasn't sure that she liked it. She wiped her damp palms on her pajama pants and tried to avoid Mama's piercing stare. "You mean at that new school of yours? Who has been bullying you?" The sigh that followed was loaded with disappointment. "Honestly. Big fancy school like that, you'd think they'd have better policies in place to monitor student interaction. . . ."

"It's nobody at school," Suraya said quickly. If Mama got on the topic of What Schools Should Be Doing to Better Serve Teachers and Students they would never get anywhere. She watched as Mama's expression switched from irritation to one of confusion.

"Then who . . ." A look of understanding began to dawn. "You know," she began in that overly casual way that meant she was thinking very hard about how to be casual, "girl friendships can be very complicated. There's often an element of competition and insecurity about it. Girls can be very catty. . . ."

Was she talking about Jing? With a creeping sense of horror, Suraya realized that she was. "It's not Jing!" she cried, aghast at the very thought. That Mama would think of frank, funny Jing as a mean girl! The idea would have made her laugh if she wasn't busy tying herself up in knots.

"Then what, Suraya?" Mama's brows had snapped back together. The irritation was back now, and it had bled into her voice, adding a harsh sharpness to its edges.

Tell her, Suraya, she told herself firmly. *You have to tell her.*

"I'm being bullied by a ghost," she blurted out.

Mama's eyebrows shot up so high they almost disappeared into her hairline.

"A . . . ghost?"

Mama didn't believe her. *And why should she? You sound ridiculous.*

Suraya couldn't tell anymore whether that was Pink's voice or her own in her head, and it frightened her. Her heart sank right down to the very soles of her feet. She wished she could reach out and pluck the words right out of the air, erase them somehow so that this whole thing had never happened.

"What kind of ghost?"

The words sent her flying back to her senses. Mama's eyes were carefully blank, giving away nothing. Was she serious? Was she making fun? It was hard to tell.

"A . . . a ghost who sometimes looks like a grasshopper?" Her uncertainty made every sentence come out sounding like a question. "He says my grandmother gave him to me? After she died?"

Was it her imagination, or did a ripple just pass through Mama's face, as though a breeze had tweaked the curtain aside, just an inch?

"Your grandmother," she said. She hadn't moved, but the air around them suddenly felt thicker, harder to suck in.

"That's . . . that's what he said?" Mama motioned for her to continue, and she poured out the whole story, from meeting Pink for the first time when she was five, to Jing's run-in with the bullies, to the nightmares. "He says I won't be rid of him so easily," she said, rubbing her aching head. "But I don't think I can take much more, Mama. I'm scared."

The silence was a long one, and each second of it made Suraya's heart fold into itself, until she thought it might disappear altogether.

Then from her mother came a long, soft sigh. "A pelesit," she murmured, as if to herself. "Of course, Ma, up to your usual tricks even in the end, curse you."

"Tricks? Curse?" Suraya swallowed back a sudden lump that had appeared in her throat and didn't seem to want to go away.

Mama straightened up in her seat and turned to look at Suraya. Her gaze was unwavering, and when she spoke, her tone was serious. "Listen to me, Suraya. Your grandmother had dangerous ideas and played with dangerous knowledge. This . . . thing that is bothering you . . . it was not made for good, do you understand? It is an evil thing, a dark thing."

"Evil?" Suraya frowned. "I don't think Pink's evil, Mama. He just loves me too much."

"I don't think it's a good idea to depend too much on his love," her mother said. "Not when all that love is doing is hurting you." Mama sighed a deep, exhausted sigh, gathering up the exercise books and stacking them neatly in one corner of the table. "I'm going to get some help. This requires an expert."

She placed a hand on Suraya's shoulder and bent down to look her in the eyes. "We will solve this problem," Mama told her. "Don't worry."

But as she walked back to her room, Suraya did worry. Because she'd looked back and seen Mama's face. Unguarded, the curtains had been flung open, the glass cracked from side to side.

Mama was very, very frightened indeed.

TWENTY-ONE

ghost

THE NEXT DAY, the ghost watched the scene unfold from his perch, right at the corner of where walls met ceiling, cloaked in shadows.

The coffee table was laid with what he recognized as Mama's good lacy table runner, the one Suraya had "borrowed" once to wrap around her waist like a fancy princess skirt; that had earned her an earful when Mama found out. The carefully polished silver tray on top of it held plates of treats, a large red-capped jar of murukku, and the ornate cups with matching saucers that they only used for guests.

He had been listening the whole time, of course. He wasn't sure who Mama's "expert help" would turn out to be, but he'd seen many "spiritual practitioners" in his time, and they were almost always true to type: men with beards that ran the spectrum from black to white, from those who truly wanted to help and believed they could to those who wanted nothing more than the feel of crisp new notes of money in their palms.

This one was . . . different.

Pink crept carefully out of the darkness to get a better look at the plump, bespectacled man who sat in the living room now, nibbling on leftover Eid cookies and drinking sweet, hot tea. "Delicious," he said, as he reached for yet another one of the biscuits stacked on the delicate china platter, the layers of flaky dough making a satisfying crunch as he bit down to get to its sticky center. "What do you call these things?"

"Heong peng."

"Ah yes, a Perak specialty, am I right?"

Mama nodded stiffly. "I grew up eating them; I am very fond of them."

She called him Encik Ali. He had a sprinkling of hair on his upper lip and chin that could probably pass as a mustache and beard if you were feeling kind enough that day, and he was wearing round glasses with thin black frames and smudged lenses, and a pale gray jubah. Cookie crumbs and stray bits of murukku nestled in its folds. Suraya sat in the chair opposite, hands folded in her lap, pale and watchful. Pink searched her face for some sign of what she thought about all of this and saw nothing but skepticism behind her mask of politeness. He couldn't help himself; he felt his nonexistent heart swell with pride. *That's my girl. Don't fall for their nonsense.*

"Mmm, mmm." Encik Ali nodded after he'd heard Suraya's story, mopping the dregs of tea from the corners of his mouth with the flowery napkins Mama had made Suraya dig up from deep within a kitchen drawer. "It does seem to be a classic case of pelesit, yes. And from your mother, you say?" He turned to Mama, his eyebrows quirked questioningly. "She was a . . . practitioner of . . . those types of things?"

"She was a witch," Mama said flatly. "And she could not stop even if she tried. It's part of why I left, a long time ago."

"Indeed, indeed," the man muttered, nodding again. "And no one can blame you for it. It cannot have been an easy childhood. . . ."

"Back to the matter at hand," Mama said, raising her voice to just shy of outright rudeness. "What can we do, Encik Ali? Can you help my daughter? She is a good girl, a girl who does as she's told. She doesn't deserve to be swept up in . . . all of this."

"Mmm," he said again, scratching the patchy hair on his chin. "I believe I can, yes. You know I am a pawang, and we have certain powers. Some people call a pawang hujan when the drought hurts their crops and they want to call upon the rain. Some people call a pawang buaya when a crocodile threatens the safety of their villages and it needs handling.

Me, I am a pawang hantu, and they call me when they have problems of a . . . spiritual nature. So you did the right thing."

Pawang hantu? Pink felt a sudden cold prickling tiptoe up his back. He had not expected this man, this bumbling, genial, crumb-dusted man, to really be able to handle ghosts and monsters. Could he really do this? Could he really be Pink's downfall?

Was this . . . fear?

The pawang turned to Suraya. "Can you withstand a few more days of this, child? Are you strong enough, brave enough?"

"I think so," Suraya said. "I hope so."

"Mmm, very well then." The pawang dabbed at his shiny forehead with his napkin. "The full moon is in five days."

"That's when I usually feed him," she said. "For . . . for the binding."

The pawang nodded. "That is when whatever rituals and incantations we use are most powerful, you see. And he needs you then, no matter how angry he may be with you. Your blood is the only thing keeping him tied to this world. Your blood is the bait." A stray piece of murukku fell out of a fold onto his lap; he picked it up and absentmindedly popped it into his mouth. "A full moon is a marvelous and fearsome thing," he said, chewing thoughtfully.

"My mother used to say the same thing," Mama said, then closed her mouth quickly, as though she'd said too much.

"I don't doubt it," the pawang said quietly, his voice all gentle sympathy. "But it is also a tricky thing, moonlight. It's like adding sugar to a cake. Add a little and it makes a raw mixture palatable. Add a little more, and an okay cake becomes great. A little more and a great cake becomes a culinary masterpiece, enough to bring grown men to tears. A little more . . . and all is ruined."

"What does that mean?" Suraya asked, and Pink wondered the same.

"Only that we must be careful," the pawang said, turning his warm smile on her.

"Will she be all right?" For the first time, there was hesitance in Mama's voice. "Will it . . . will it hurt her?"

"No, it shouldn't hurt. Not for her."

Suraya looked at him through narrowed eyes. "Will it hurt him?"

In that moment, Pink loved her so hard he thought the cavity where his heart ought to be would burst.

"Him?" The pawang raised an eyebrow at this as he carefully set his teacup back down on the coffee table. There was a clink as glass hit glass. "Surely you mean *it*, child."

"I mean him," she said stubbornly. Pink noticed Mama's

lips, now pressed together so tightly a piece of paper couldn't
have passed between them. "What will happen to him?"

The question seemed to leave the pawang nonplussed.
"Well. He would go away."

It was at that moment that you might have heard a sharp
hiss from the darkest corner of the room, if you were listening.

"Forever?"

"If we do it right."

The room suddenly seemed darker. Where it had been
bright afternoon sunshine just seconds ago, clouds now
loomed on the horizon, dark and angry and flickering with
lightning. Mama got up then, crossing the room to close the
windows against the gathering storm.

"Will it hurt him?" Suraya asked again.

The wind turned the rain into sharp, thin whips that lashed
unceasingly against the tin roof; it turned the branches of the
trees outside into fists that pounded hard against the window-
panes.

The pawang smiled. "If we do it right," he said again, and
behind those smudged lenses Pink thought he detected a peculiar gleam.

Suraya shivered, and Pink shivered with her.

"Do not worry, child," the pawang said kindly. "I will keep
you safe. No harm will come your way. But this thing that

haunts you . . . it will keep hurting you unless we banish it, get rid of it forever. Do you understand?"

She waited a long time to answer, and in the minutes that ticked by, Pink wanted to yell out, tell her that he would not hurt her again, that he could not help himself sometimes but that he would try so hard, so much harder than he was trying now. He could not imagine a world in which he could never see her or be near her again, and he did not want to.

"Encik Ali is asking you a question, Suraya." Mama's teacher voice cut through the silence, the note of authority unmistakable. It was a voice that demanded you sit up straight and pay attention and keep your eyes on your own paper. It was a voice that demanded answers.

"Yes," Suraya said softly. "I understand."

Outside, the wind howled as if it were a wild beast that someone had stabbed in the heart.

TWENTY-TWO

girl

SURAYA LAY IN her bed after the pawang had left and thought for a long, long time. She thought about the smell, and the nightmares, and of Jing's pale face and purple bruises. She thought about whispered conversations under the covers, and warm hugs at bedtime, and first friendships, and true friendships. She thought about that strange gleam in the pawang's eyes, the shiver of fear that had run a cold finger down her spine when he spoke. And most of all, she thought about forever, a word that got colder and harder and more unforgiving the longer it sat in her head.

The shadows were long by the time she sat up. Sweat made her long hair stick to the back of her neck, and she gathered it impatiently up into a sloppy ponytail.

"Pink," she whispered.

It was the first time she'd said his name in days, and it tasted strange and bittersweet and familiar on her tongue.

The storm was dying out now, and the wind had lost most of its ferocity; the only answer was its whimpers outside her window.

"Pink," she said again. This time her voice was clearer, surer.

The shadows in the corners of the room started to grow larger and darker, as if they were gathering themselves together.

"I know you're here, Pink," Suraya said. "You're always here. Come out and talk to me."

The shadows in the corners flickered for a second, the way they do when a breeze plays with a candle flame.

Then he was there, not as his true form, but as a grasshopper on her windowsill. Behind him, the sky was lit up with the fiery flames of sunset, and the shadow he cast was huge and vaguely sinister.

"Hello, Pink."

He didn't speak, so she did instead. "You're probably wondering why I called you."

"I assume it was to say your final goodbye," he said, and she winced at the unfamiliar harshness in his voice.

"It wasn't my idea," she said.

"Yet I missed the bit where you launched a passionate

protest," he snapped. "Or perhaps it was smothered by all the betrayal in the air."

"Betrayal?" She stared at him, mouth agape, eyes filling with furious tears. "You're the one who's been spending all your time trying to hurt my friend! Trying to hurt me!"

Beneath her feet, she felt a shudder. The room began to tremble, the picture frames clattering slightly against the walls upon which they were hung, the art supplies on her desk clicking and clacking against each other with every movement.

When he spoke again, Pink's voice was a deep rumble. "You dropped me as soon as you had another human to be your companion! Me, who has been by your side since you were barely old enough to walk! Me, who has been with you through everything! Who has . . . who has loved you through everything!" The last words flew out of his mouth in a roar that shook the room so hard that Suraya grabbed onto her bedstead, sure she was about to be sent flying across the room. Pens and pencils and books and papers fell or fluttered to the ground. The sound was deafening.

Pink paused to catch his breath, panting slightly.

On her bed, Suraya sobbed quietly, her face buried in her hands. With every heave of her little chest, Pink thought his heart would break—if he had one, that is.

Look at me, he told her.

It took a while for her to obey. When she did, the fear in her eyes made him tremble.

She'd never looked at him like that before.

Pink let out a long, slow sigh, as if he was releasing all the anger from his little body. Then he hopped onto the bed beside her and laid a gentle arm against her leg.

I am sorry, he whispered. *I did not mean to hurt you. I did not like to do it. But my anger billowed and swelled and grew inside me, and, like the wild thing it is, it lashed out when it was wounded. I could not stop it.*

"Did you enjoy it?"

He looked down at his feet. He could not help feeling ashamed of himself. *I did.*

She nodded. "It felt like you did." There was no note of blame or anger in her voice, just the tiny tremble of leftover tears.

I will not do it anymore, he told her. *Or at least . . . I will try not to.*

"It's okay," she said. "It's in your nature. It's hard to go against what you were meant to be."

I was meant to be your friend. His voice was sad.

"You will always be my friend, Pink."

He looked at her intently. *Then why does this sound like a goodbye?*

"It isn't. Not yet." Suraya rubbed the tears from her face and sat up, scooping Pink up in her palm and bringing him close to her. "Listen, Pink. In five days, at the full moon, they're going to make you go away forever, and they won't do it gently, I know it. I could see it in that man's eyes."

Child. He leaned close and nuzzled her cheek. *Child, what can you do in the face of your elders? How can you stop them? You are wise, but still so young.*

He watched her jaw set, that spark of determination light in her eyes, and he knew she would not listen.

"Fortune favors the bold," she reminded him.

He had to smile.

All right, he said. *What do we do?*

TWENTY-THREE

girl

THE PAWANG HAD come into town driving a trim little camper that he'd parked on the very edge of the village, where the neat, orderly paddy fields butted up against an unapologetically wild, unruly tangle of forest, "so as to keep out of everyone's way," he'd said. Such was the demand for his services as a handler of unruly spirits that he saw no use in settling down in one place. "I bring my home with me wherever I go," he'd told Suraya's mother earnestly as he left. "And I help whoever I can, insha Allah."

So, even in the inky darkness of midnight under a cloud-clogged sky, it was easy enough for Suraya and Pink to sneak past Mama snoring gently in her usual seat in front of the flickering TV screen and out of the house, through the paths and shortcuts as familiar as the lines on her own palm, to where the battered camper stood, a faint light glowing from one window.

From his perch on Suraya's shoulder, Pink sniffed. *Explain to me why we are doing this again?*

"I told you," Suraya whispered back. "There's something about this guy that just doesn't feel right. I want to know what he's up to."

Be careful, he told her. But she didn't answer; she was too busy sidling up against the walls of the camper, stretching on her tiptoes to peek into its streaky windows.

They are too high for you, he pointed out helpfully. *And anyway, the curtains are closed. You would not be able to see.*

She glared at him. "All right, then, Mr. Helpful, you go in there and tell me what you see."

He sniffed again and hopped off her shoulder and toward the door of the camper. In the darkness, she could just make out his little body as it wriggled through the keyhole and disappeared.

He was gone a long time. Suraya shifted her weight from one foot to the other as she waited, wiping the sweat that dripped from her brow with the back of her hand, trying to ignore the shadows that seemed to waver and shift as she watched, the rustling and whispering that wafted from the undergrowth. *It's just the trees,* she told herself. Just the wind blowing through the branches. Nothing to worry about.

Then she heard a sound that had nothing to do with the trees at all, or the screeches of the insects that sang loudly in the still night.

The click of a door handle.

She turned just in time to see the door of the camper swing slowly, silently open.

There was nobody there. There was nothing but the empty doorway, faintly illuminated by the light inside the camper.

Suraya felt her body begin to tremble all over, and she turned away from the yawning emptiness, ready to run.

Suraya.

She looked back. "Pink?"

She felt the familiar, reassuring tap of his little feet as he landed on her shoulder. *It's all right. There's nobody here. He's out.*

Suraya took a deep, shaky breath, trying to steady her thundering heart. "Excellent. Now let's go see what's going on."

She climbed up the steps of the camper slowly, partly to make sure she didn't make a sound, partly because her knees still felt decidedly wobbly.

Inside, the camper was tidy, organized, and achingly, disappointingly normal. The pawang had left a small lamp on, its fluorescent glow straining to light its surroundings. A cursory glance through the contents of the cupboards revealed a small space dedicated to basic cookery ingredients—a little carafe of canola oil, glass jars with salt and sugar beached along the sides, bottles of sauces in every shade and spice variant, from the caramel darkness of sweet soy sauce to the flaming red of a sauce made with tiny, dangerously hot bird's-eye chilis. The rest held row upon row of leather- and clothbound books, some new, some with flakes of material peeling off the spines like sunburned skin. There were no photographs or ornaments to provide some insight into his solitary life, and no little messes; no papers strewn carelessly over tabletops, no crumpled piles of dirty clothes left to fester on the floor.

"A place for everything, and everything in its place," she whispered to herself. It was something Mama often said when Suraya's room started getting out of control; she didn't think the pawang had ever been out of control in his life.

Pink had peeled himself from her shoulder and gone exploring on his own, and she'd almost forgotten where he was until she heard a small gasp from the bedroom.

Suraya. Come here.

"Hmm?" She ran her hand over the multicolored spines of the books, trying to make out their titles in the dim light. "In a minute, Pink."

Now. Something in his voice made her look up. *You need to see this.*

She walked down the narrow little corridor toward him.

The first thing she noticed was the little bed, perfectly made, the blue bedspread folded so neatly and so tightly over the corners that each one was as sharp as a knife's edge.

The second thing she noticed was Pink, sitting squarely in the center of that smooth blue bedspread, his mouth set in a grim line, staring at something right behind her.

The third thing she noticed, as she slowly turned around, was a wall filled with row upon row of shelves, from floor to ceiling, fitting neatly around the narrow sliver of doorway she'd just come through.

The fourth thing she noticed was the jars.

There were so many of them, lined up along each shelf like sentinels, tall jars, thin jars, fat jars, each made of clear glass with a silver top screwed on tight.

And inside each one, a dark shape.

Suraya frowned and took a step closer. One jar held what she recognized as a musang, the type of civet that often scrabbled lightly across their roof in the light of the moon, curled up with its eyes shut tight. One held an owl with downy gray feathers and long talons that ended in wicked points; its eyes too were closed. One—and it was at this point that Suraya began to tremble so hard that she felt her teeth tap-tap-tapping against each other in her mouth—held a baby, completely naked, its skin tinged a sickly green, its ears tapering at the tips, the sharp points of tiny fangs resting against its bottom lip as it slept. And more, so many more things she couldn't even recognize, the stuff of spite and nightmares.

Taking a deep breath, Suraya bent forward to peer more closely into one of the jars in which there rested something she couldn't quite make out.

Two tiny eyes peered back.

They sat in a tiny face, and the face belonged to a tiny figure, no bigger than the tip of her little finger. It was black all over, and its little limbs ended in wickedly clawed fingers and toes, and it looked at her without blinking.

She had often read about little girls who found imps and fairies in the woods and made friends with them. This little imp did not look like it wanted to make friends.

As she watched, it narrowed its eyes, bared a mouth full of sharp, pointed fangs at her, and hissed with such venom that its glass prison shook.

She backed away quickly, her hands shaking.

Row upon row of jars, row upon row of dark shapes that had begun to move restlessly against their glass confines. And they were all staring right at her.

Suraya felt her heart pounding in her ears. Each stare pierced her skin like a thousand tiny pinpricks, and yet somehow she couldn't move.

Run, she heard a voice whisper, like the rustling of old leaves, then another, then another, then another, louder and louder until the rustle built itself up into a roar. *RUN RUN RUN RUN RUN RUN RUN RUN RUN.*

Suraya. Pink's voice, urgent and scared, brought her abruptly back to herself. *I suggest you do as they tell you.*

And with her ghost clinging to her left shoulder, Suraya raced out of the camper and back home, the words still echoing in her ear with every step.

In the shadows of the restless banana trees, the pawang watched her go. Behind the smudged lenses of his glasses, his eyes gleamed.

TWENTY-FOUR

ghost

SURAYA LAY CURLED up in her bed, and she couldn't stop shaking.

Pink was worried about her, and it just about killed him that he had no idea how to help her. "What were they?" she asked, over and over again. "What were those . . . those creatures?"

Pink sat quiet and unmoving on the windowsill, watching as ribbons of sunlight slowly began to lick the corners of the neighboring houses, thinking about those muffled whispers, the pointed stare of hundreds of beady little eyes.

All manner of dark things, he said quietly. *There was a bajang—that's the civet you saw, that's the shape it takes. It can cause a type of madness, a delirium, to whoever its master sends it to torment.*

"Its master?" Suraya stared at him. "You mean the pawang?"

Yes. And it was not the only one. There were more. Pink sighed. *The owl is another form taken by the langsuir. She is a type of banshee, preying on pregnant mothers, though I suppose if you have the right skill, she can prey on whoever you want her to. The baby, that was a toyol, a child spirit who can be used by its master to cause all sorts of mischief.*

"And the little one?"

That was a polong. A spirit bound by blood, like me. It can render its victims deaf and blind to their surroundings, totally unconscious of their own actions, ranting and raving like a lunatic. And there was more than one of those, more than I could count.

Suraya buried her head in her hands. "I don't understand. Why is he doing this? What does he want with those . . . those creatures?"

It seems to me that the man is a Collector, Pink said calmly. *I have heard of his kind. They are not content with small, petty bad magics as your grandmother was. They desire greater things, and they use their spirits like slaves.*

"What kind of things do they want?" Suraya asked. Her voice trembled.

Pink's sigh was long and weary. *Anything you could think of, really,* he said. *Theft. Assault. Murder. Imagine being in control of polongs and pelesits, toyols and bajangs and langsuirs. An army of ghosts and monsters. You would be almost unstoppable.*

"But what does he want you for? Doesn't he have enough?" she said, her voice rising and tinged with frustration. "And you're bound by blood too. How can he do that? I thought that was the whole point, that you couldn't belong to anyone else."

Power is an addiction. A small taste is often enough for people to crave another, and then another, and then another, and those who have it will do anything to get more of it.

"And he called himself RELIGIOUS!" She drove her fist into the mattress, pounding it over and over again, punctuating her words with their soft, satisfying thumps. "How can he just USE religion like that? What kind of monster does that?"

He is not the first, nor will he be the last. Pink turned to look at her, his voice gentle. *You will find, child, that there are many monsters in this world who hide their darkness beneath a mask of piety. Call yourself a religious man and nobody will question you; do it well enough and you can stab them in the back, again and again and again, while they nod and say it is all for their own good.*

Suraya shuddered. "We can't let him collect you too."

How do you propose we stop him?

"We'll think of something."

Pink shook his head, but said nothing. He just kept staring

out at the world, now alive with fresh morning sunlight and new possibilities.

In the distance, they heard the front door slam shut; Mama, off to the village school for another day of teaching.

"We could run away."

No. He didn't even bother to look at her.

"Why not? If we ran away, somewhere he couldn't find us, you'd be safe. You wouldn't be part of his nasty old collection. And I could take care of you. We could take care of each other."

There was a long pause. *Suraya, that is no life for a child. A life spent hiding and running, a life spent scraping and scrambling just to survive each day. You cannot be serious.*

She set her little chin and looked straight at him, his brave, brave girl, his master. "I am," she told him firmly. "I don't see how there can be any other way."

And what about food? What about a place to live? What about money? What about school? What about Jing? What about your mother? He fired the questions at her rapidly, never waiting for an answer. *Please, Suraya. No more foolishness.*

When she spoke again, her voice was small and sad. "And what about you?"

Before he could answer, the tinny ding of the doorbell echoed through the house.

Suraya frowned. "Who can that be? Nobody ever comes around this time of day."

Or at all, mumbled Pink caustically, rubbing his aching head.

Pretending not to hear him, Suraya made her way to the front door and opened it just the tiniest of cracks.

It was Jing.

"Hullo," Jing said, then stopped, rubbing the cast on one arm awkwardly with her other hand. She was dressed in her school pinafore, her backpack slung over her shoulder, a white-robed Princess Leia keychain dangling off the zipper.

What is she doing here? Pink hissed. Surely even in their troubles, they need not include her as well?

"What are you doing here?" Suraya echoed.

"I waited for Ma to leave after dropping me off at school, then I took the bus here. You weren't kidding, man, it really takes damn long." Jing peered at her anxiously. "You okay? You haven't been in school so long already. I was getting worried."

"I'm . . ." Suraya hesitated.

Tell her you're fine, Pink said quietly, straight into her ear. *Tell her to go home.*

"Why don't you come in?" she said instead, opening the door wider and gesturing inside.

Pink sighed.

Inside, Jing spent an inordinate amount of time walking around Suraya's small room, running her hands and eyes over everything, from the little bookshelf beneath the window, to the bed with its faded floral sheets, to the wooden desk covered in pots of pens and pencils, though the notebook was now firmly locked away in a drawer.

Suraya stood by the door, her arms crossed tight across her chest. Nobody ever came into her room, and Pink knew how vulnerable it made her feel to let Jing in, taking in everything with her sharp little eyes.

"Let's go get a snack," she said finally, holding the door open. "You must be hungry." It was a safe bet, Pink thought. As far as he could tell, Jing was always hungry.

"Okay," Jing said.

"Come on."

"Okay! I'm coming." Jing made her way hurriedly to the door.

"Hurry up," Suraya tossed behind her shoulder to Pink.

"What are you talking about? I'm already out here." Jing's face wore a frown of confusion, and she was so busy staring at Suraya that she never noticed the little grasshopper leaping past her toward the kitchen, where the snacks were waiting.

Outside, the storm clouds began to gather.

They sat together on the cold concrete of the porch, passing a jar of iced gem biscuits back and forth between them, listening to the crash of thunder and watching the rain pelt and pound the earth. The biscuits had been Suraya's favorite ever since she was a little girl, and they always had them at home; Pink could still remember the old days when she'd called them biskut aiskrim, thick vanilla discs the size of a button covered in a pure sugar swirl of green or white or pink that looked exactly like a dollop of ice cream.

"So what's going on?" Jing had to yell over the drumming of the rain on the porch's tin roof. "I know something's wrong."

"How do you know?" Suraya yelled back.

"It's written all over your face."

There was a rumble of thunder, farther away now than it had been just a few minutes ago. The storm was moving on.

"It's . . . complicated."

"So what." Jing shrugged, taking a handful of biscuits and passing the jar back. "Look, if I can make it through reading all three Lord of the Rings books and still keep the characters straight without my head exploding, then I can handle your life." She bit off a swirl of pink icing and chewed it thoughtfully. "Especially if your story has any Aragorn types."

Pink thought it felt good to hear Suraya laugh. It felt good to see her smile. What didn't feel good was the realization that she hadn't been like this with him, not for a good long while.

He sidled up to her ear. *Tell her,* he said.

"Are you sure?"

"Sure about what?" She'd barely been here half an hour, and already the look of confusion on Jing's face was becoming a permanent feature.

Tell her. Maybe she can help.

"But what if she doesn't believe me?"

Jing wasn't chewing anymore, and her confusion was tinged with worry.

"What's going on, Sooz? Who're you talking to?"

The storm was almost gone by now; all that was left was a stubborn drizzle and a chill in the air that made Suraya shiver. "You're going to think I'm crazy," she said, half laughing.

In an instant, Jing was next to her, her arm around Suraya's shoulder. "You can tell me anything," she said seriously, her eyes earnest behind her glasses. "I am your friend lah, silly. The Chewie to your Han. Let me help you."

Pink didn't know what Chewies and Hans were. He just knew he wanted to be Suraya's friend too. And that meant letting Jing in, no matter how much it hurt.

Suraya took a deep breath. "Okay," she said. "Here goes."

She talked for what felt like a long time, until the chill in the air had long disappeared.

A shadow fell across Jing's face, making it hard to read.

"Well?" The nervousness in Suraya's voice was palpable.

"Where is he now?" Jing asked. Her tone gave nothing away.

"Here." Pink hopped from her shoulder onto Suraya's open palm.

"That's him?" Jing's hand went to her cast almost protectively. "That's your . . . your friend?"

"You don't believe me?" Suraya bit down hard on her bottom lip to keep it from trembling, and Pink watched as a drop of blood welled up from beneath her teeth.

This is ridiculous. The air shimmered around him, and for an instant there he was, in all his monstrous glory, scaled and horned. The glow of the late afternoon sun made it look as if his skin flickered with fire.

Then the moment was over, and there was nothing but the tiny green grasshopper on Suraya's palm.

Jing blinked. "Okay," she said quietly. "Okay. I'm convinced."

Suraya sucked in a deep, noisy breath, as if someone had let go of their iron grip on her lungs and she could finally take in some desperately needed air. "Oh thank goodness, because I don't think we can do this on our own."

"That's me." Jing smiled a nervous smile, still cradling her injured arm. "The third musketeer." Her eyes never left Pink, who stayed perfectly still in Suraya's hand.

"Well then." Suraya looked from one best friend to the other and took a deep breath. "Let's get to work."

TWENTY-FIVE

 *girl*

"OKAY," JING SAID, pacing up and down in Suraya's little room. "The first thing we need to do is find out his origin story." She jerked her head in Pink's general direction.

"What?" Suraya stared at her. "We have no time for stories. We need a plan."

Jing stopped pacing and sighed. "Have you learned nothing from Star Wars? The only way Luke could defeat Darth Vader was by knowing how he *became* Darth Vader. When he knew that, he could figure out how to defeat him, by tapping into the person he used to be." She coughed. "So we need to know where . . . Pink . . . came from."

You must know my past to determine my future? Pink rubbed his chin thoughtfully. *Spoken like a philosopher.*

"He says you sound like a philosopher." Suraya was sure

Pink could speak directly to Jing if he really wanted to. He just didn't want to.

"Or someone who watches a lot of movies." Jing flopped down hard on the bed, making Pink jump. "So spill, little demon. Tell us how you were made, and who made you."

Tell her to kindly not address me as "little demon." I have a name.

"His name is Pink, Jing."

"All right, Pink." Jing rolled her eyes. "Stop being such a nerf herder and just answer the question."

What is a nerf herder? Why does she speak in tongues?

"Pink." Suraya shut her eyes and massaged her aching temples. "Please just tell us."

Tell you?

"Tell *us* where you came from."

There was the tiniest of pauses before he replied. *I came from your grandmother, of course. She made me.*

Suraya regarded him with narrowed eyes. "What did he say?" Jing whispered. "You're making your level ten angry face. The last time you made this face it was because Shuba tried to copy you during the geography test, remember or not? That scolding you gave her! I think her right ear was almost about to fall off. . . ."

"Shush, Jing." Suraya kept her gaze steadily on Pink, who

seemed to be working very hard not to look at her. "Pink, I know what it's like when someone is trying to avoid telling me something. I live with my mother, remember? Now talk. Where did you come from?"

It was a long time before Pink spoke again. *To make a pelesit,* he said finally, *one would need to dig up the corpse of a recently deceased child and place it on an anthill.*

Was it Suraya's imagination, or was the air suddenly weighed down by a sudden chill?

Then, when the scurrying feet and sharp teeth of the ants make the dead child cry out, you would bite his tongue from his mouth, say a special incantation, and bury it where three roads meet, for three nights.

By the time Pink's story ended, Suraya's tongue felt like sandpaper, and her mouth was so dry that it took her a minute to form the words for Jing's benefit.

"That's how that thing was made?" Jing's eyes were wide. "Someone BIT a dead kid's TONGUE out of his MOUTH?"

"He's not a thing. He's a . . . he's Pink. And yes, that's how he was made."

"AWESOME."

Suraya turned back to Pink and took a deep breath. "And it was my grandmother that made you?"

Pink's voice was gentle. *Yes. It was the witch.*

It felt like someone had wrapped her chest in metal bands and was squeezing them tight, so that she could hardly breathe. "You told me that was *what* she was. But you never told me this was *how* she was."

You never needed to know.

Jing was peering closely at Pink, her face alive with horrified excitement. "A dead kid's tongue," she breathed. "Cooooooooooooool."

"Jing!"

"Sorry!" She straightened up, her expression apologetic. "Sorry. I know this is a lot for you to take."

Suraya tried her best to take a deep breath. There was no time for this; no time for confusion and racing thoughts and taking apart her entire family history. "Enough of that. Now that we know, how do we use that to help us keep Pink out of that pawang's slimy clutches?"

Jing frowned in concentration. "Well, if it . . . I mean he, sorry, he . . . if he came from the grave, maybe that's where he needs to go. You know. Back."

"Back?" Suraya frowned. "You mean, like, bury him?"

"Ya!" Jing pushed her glasses up from where they'd slipped down her nose in her enthusiasm. "If you think about it right, he's like . . . a missing piece. Maybe reuniting him with the rest of his old self will give him peace. What do you think?" She turned to Pink, her eyebrows raised.

You would return me to the grave?

"You'd be safe there. Nobody would be able to hurt you. Maybe . . . maybe you would like it?" Suraya turned to him, her face unsure. "Maybe it would be like going home?"

There was a pause.

All right, he said softly. *All right. Let us try.*

And then the doorbell rang once again.

Nobody had gates or fences marking the borders of their gardens in Suraya's village; since everyone was friends and neighbors, nobody saw any reason to keep visitors out instead of welcoming them in.

So there was nothing to stop the pawang from marching up to Suraya's home and ringing the bell, and nothing to prepare Suraya for the shock of seeing his face looming near one of the small slivers of windows on either side of the door, trying his best to peer through the multihued panels of stained glass.

In her pocket, Pink froze.

The pawang's roaming eyes met hers, and he smiled, showing rows of perfectly straight white teeth.

"Assalamualaikum," he called. "Won't you open the door?"

Suraya's heart began to pound. "I can't," she managed. "My mom isn't home and I'm not supposed to open the door to strangers."

The pawang laughed, a strangely high, light sound that carried through the glass window and grated on Suraya's every nerve. "I'm hardly a stranger, child," he said. "I've been in your home and eaten your food. I'm your friend. Let me in." The stained glass distorted his smiling mouth so that it looked like a wide, gaping maw.

In her pocket, Pink shook his head frantically. Suraya wished her heart would stop beating so loud.

"It's hard to talk to you through this barrier, my dear," the pawang continued, his voice silky and wheedling. "Why don't you open it? Just a little? All I want is to have a little conversation."

Suraya squeezed her eyes shut and remembered a thousand wicked little eyes, staring straight into her soul.

Outside, the pawang sighed. "Very well then. I suppose I'll come back when your mother is home." He leaned forward then, so his lips were right against the crack where the door met the wall, so that his voice, when it came, was whispering almost directly into Suraya's ear.

"You should trust me, you know," he said softly. "Everything

I do is for your own good. And trying to defy me won't help you at all."

Suraya stood frozen to the spot, her hands cold and clammy, her heart racing as if it would explode straight out of her chest.

The pawang straightened up. "All right then," he said, his tone cheerful. "See you another time!" And he walked off without a backward glance.

Jing crept out of Suraya's room, where she'd stayed for fear of being found playing hooky. "Who was that?"

Suraya wiped the sweat from her brow and tried to pry loose the cold fingers of fear that clenched at her heart. Pink hopped up from her pocket to her shoulder, nuzzling his tiny head against her pale cheek. "He's the reason we need to figure out a plan as soon as possible."

"Okay," Jing said, fishing her phone out of her bag and carefully avoiding Suraya's gaze while she called up the search engine. Jing rarely used her phone or even talked about it in front of her friend. Long ago, when Suraya had been pouting about not getting the same golden-haired Barbies the other girls spent hours dressing and undressing, her mother had sat her down and explained to her that the world was divided between the Haves, the Have-Nots, and those who

Have-Enough-to-Get-By. "That's us," Mama had said. "We have just enough to live. Not enough for the luxuries others have. Understand?"

"Understand," Suraya had said then. And she did understand. She understood that a phone was a thing only Haves could really afford, and that Jing was a Have, and that knowing how much more she had compared to Suraya made her uncomfortable—maybe even a little guilty—even though Suraya herself didn't care. What she did care about right now in this moment was finding the best way to help Pink, and if Jing's phone could help them do that, all the better.

"The first thing we need to do is figure out where you come from, Pink. Sooz, do you know where your grandma lived?"

Suraya shook her head, a hot flush creeping over her cheeks. "I, umm, didn't even know I had a grandma until I was, like, five. My mother never talks about her." She couldn't help but read a thousand different judgments in the lines of Jing's frown as she stared at the phone, waiting for her app to load.

"Okay, okay, never mind," Jing said. "Small matter. We can still figure it out. Does the thing have any clues?"

"Stop calling him that! His name is Pink."

Suraya watched Pink thankfully ignore the jab from Jing and instead mull over her question. It took a while. Finally he spoke, *It's been so long since I last thought about the witch,*

*longer still since I set foot in any of my former homes. The
witch moved about often. She was not one to stay in one place
for long, nor would she have been welcome. But at the last village, in the place she drew her last breath . . . there were jambu
trees in the garden, and a round pond with tiny fish flitting in
its depths. And we were close enough to the mosque to see the
blue dome and the minarets from the kitchen window, and to
mark time by the call to prayer.*

Suraya relayed this to Jing, who sighed as she tapped away
on the phone screen. "O-kay, thank you for that. I mean, I was
hoping for something more along the lines of, like, the name of
a town, or a state, or even a landmark besides, like, fruit trees
and a mosque with a blue dome, since I'm 99 percent sure that
every other kampung in Malaysia has one of those. . . ."

"Maybe my mom has some old letters lying around," Suraya
suggested. "I could go poke around her desk."

"It's a start," Jing said. "Let's see."

The door to Mama's room was closed. It was always closed,
whether Mama was actually in the room or not, whether
Mama was even home or not. It had been this way for as long
as Suraya could remember. The closed door, as far as she was
concerned, sent a very clear message: DO NOT ENTER.
THIS PLACE IS NOT FOR YOU.

She'd never considered ignoring that message until now.

"Well?" Jing, who bounded in and out of her own mother's room as and when she pleased—sometimes without even knocking—didn't understand Suraya's hesitation. "Open lah."

"Hold on."

"What's wrong?"

Suraya couldn't explain how much of a struggle it was to even touch the doorknob, much less turn it. THIS PLACE IS NOT FOR YOU.

"Is it stuck? Come I try." And before she could say a word, Jing reached past her and wrenched the door wide open.

For a moment, Suraya felt as if she couldn't breathe. She'd only ever caught glimpses of her mother's room before; to have this much access all at once was like suddenly being given ten Cokes to drink when she'd only ever been allowed sips of it her entire life ("Too much sugar," her mother would scoff when they passed those enticing red cans in their local supermarket). She didn't know whether to give in to the urge to drink in every little detail in huge, painful gulps, or to turn her back on it altogether and just walk away.

Fortune favors the bold, a little voice whispered in her ear. Behind her, Jing waited, as if she understood that the one to take that first step into the room had to be Suraya.

She took a deep breath.

"Well," she said over her shoulder. "Are you guys coming or what?"

And then she stepped over the threshold.

The windows were closed in Mama's room, and the curtains drawn shut, so that the sunlight struggling valiantly through its brown cotton filter cast the room in dim, sepia light. Between this and the stale, still air, it was as if time had stopped here years ago.

Suraya hadn't been sure what to expect, but if anything, she thought Mama's room might be spare and painfully neat, much like Mama herself. But this room was nothing like that at all. Instead, every inch of available space was covered in piles of . . . stuff. Books stacked precariously in piles that came up to Suraya's waist; papers peeking timidly out of the drawers they'd been shoved in; clothing in a crumpled heap on one side of the bed, where the only unoccupied space was marked by a dent in the mattress and a rumple in the sheets. The clothes Mama had worn and discarded the day before marked a trail across the room, like an adult Hansel or Gretel, leaving garments instead of bread crumbs to find their way home.

THIS PLACE IS NOT FOR YOU.

"Woooooooooow," she heard Jing breathe out beside her. "I mean, um. Where do we start?"

Suraya wasn't sure.

As if he understood, Pink spoke up. *Jing looks in there,* he said, nodding toward the closet. *I'll start on this shelf. And you will take those piles over there. Yes?* He looked up at Suraya questioningly, and she nodded, grateful for the chance to catch her breath, to have the weight of making decisions taken off her shoulders for once.

Having received her orders, Jing began rummaging around with enthusiasm, muttering under her breath as she went. "Wah," Suraya heard her say, and then "Like that also can?"

I'd tell her not to make a mess, Pink said, *but I'm not sure it makes any difference.* He turned to the high shelf that stood against one wall, filled with books and papers jammed in every which way, and Suraya sank to the floor between piles of yet more books and papers and began to sift through them.

It seemed to take forever. They found all sorts of things—romance novels with lurid covers that Suraya would never have expected her mother to read, clothes with outsized shoulder pads like relics of a bygone era, several pairs of high heels in bright colors—reds and blues and yellows and purples—covered in dust, their faux leather peeling off in strips and scraps.

By the time Suraya was done with her piles, Jing was still making new discoveries in the closet, and Pink had moved on to a stack of cardboard boxes that stood beside the shelf.

The chest of drawers, Pink told her, looking up from a pile of mismatched playing cards—Old Maid, Snap, Uno, all shoved into the same deck. *Over there.*

Suraya turned to look at the chest that stood right up against the wall, a nondescript thing of dark wood, with four rows of narrow drawers and a rattan basket on top that held an assembly of jars and bottles: Vicks VapoRub and Tiger Balm and minyak cap kapak and curling old blister packs of ibuprofen with only one or two pills still encased in their plastic prisons.

The first three drawers held nothing but reams and reams of paper—bills; cuttings from old newspapers, soft and yellowing; catalogues that had come in the mail still in their plastic wrappers, their covers promising unbelievable deals on Tupperware, dresses you could wear five different ways, and amazingly absorbent cleaning cloths; empty junk food wrappers stuffed in the spaces in between as if Mama was ashamed of consuming their contents. Suraya shuffled through all of these silently, as Jing rustled and banged in the background.

The last drawer would not open.

Suraya pulled and tugged, but all it did was reveal a couple of dark, tantalizing centimeters of itself before refusing to move any further, stubborn and unyielding. "What's in this thing?" she murmured, wiping the sweat from her brow.

"Come, let me try," Jing said, materializing by her right elbow.

I'm not sure . . . , Pink began. But it was too late. With an almighty tug and a deafening crack, the drawer broke free from whatever had been holding it back, sending Jing tumbling to the floor.

"Are you okay?" Suraya asked, hurrying to her side. Jing sat up and winced, rubbing her cast.

"I'm fine lah," she said. "Now what's inside?"

The clutter that dominated all the other parts of Mama's room had been kept far away from this tiny drawer, and it was curiously empty in comparison. There was a plain, pale blue envelope nestled at the bottom. Wicked-looking shards and splinters of wood shedding from the lock they'd apparently broken. And one other thing—a marble, large and perfectly round and shot through with swirls of blue and green and hints of gold.

Suraya picked it up. It was strangely warm in her hands, as if it had nestled in someone else's palm recently and absorbed the heat of their skin.

"Aiya, did I spoil it?" Jing's voice, high with panic, broke the spell. "You think your mom will notice? Dam—"

"Don't swear," Suraya admonished her automatically, still staring at the marble in her hands. There seemed to be something almost familiar about it.

What is in the envelope? Pink asked. His eyes too were on the orb in Suraya's hands, but if he knew what it was, he revealed nothing.

"What's in the envelope, Jing?" Suraya asked and Jing reached in.

"There's just a bunch of papers here . . . birth certificates for you and your mom, Sooz, and . . . some dude. Your dad?" She flashed Suraya an apologetic smile before she went on. "There's something else too. His . . . his death certificate."

"Oh." Suraya turned the marble over and over in her hands, concentrating hard on its smoothness and trying not to think about the piece of paper that made her father's death Official with a capital O.

"Sooz," Jing said quietly.

"What?"

"There's this bundle of letters in here."

Suraya looked up, suddenly alert. "From my grandmother?"

Jing frowned as she scanned some of the papers, each covered in the same slanting blue handwriting.

Not from your grandmother, Pink said suddenly. *To your*

grandmother. They were from your mother. I remember see-
ing them at the witch's home . . . our home . . . tucked away
in a drawer.

At the same time, Jing spoke. "These look like they're from your mom."

"They must have sent them back to her when . . . when my grandmother died."

Jing nodded. "There's an address here, we can . . ."

It was then that they all heard it: the unmistakable click of the front door handle.

Mama was home.

Quickly, Pink hissed, bounding from Suraya's shoulder to the door to keep watch. *Move. We must not be seen in here.*

Suraya's heart pounded so hard in her chest that it actually hurt, and with every beat she heard the same refrain: THIS. PLACE. IS. NOT. FOR. YOU.

Jing fished her phone out of her pocket and quickly snapped a photo of the paper in her hands—it seemed to Suraya that a camera had never sounded so loud before, and she was sure her mother would hear them—and shoved the whole bundle back in the bulging envelope. "Let's go, Sooz, before she catches us," she said breathlessly.

"Right, I'm coming," Suraya said. But as they crept quietly out of the door, she turned back and in one smooth motion slid the drawer open, grabbed the marble, and quickly tucked it into the deep pocket of her top. Then she closed the drawer as quietly as she could and left the room, pulling Mama's door shut behind her.

She didn't know why she couldn't leave that marble behind. But she knew that she couldn't.

"Suraya?" She whirled around to see Mama staring at her, her brow creased in irritated furrows. "What are you doing?"

How long had Mama been standing there? How much had she seen? Was this question a trap? Suraya's palms were damp with sweat, and she could feel her heart begin to race.

"READY OR NOT, HERE I COME!" Jing's voice boomed through the walls as she came barreling down the hallway, stopping short when she saw Suraya and Mama. "Hey, you're not hiding!" Then she stuck her good hand out and smiled her most winning, gap-toothed smile. "Hello aunty, I'm Jing Wei, Suraya's friend from school, just came to visit because I heard she wasn't well, don't worry, I have my mom's permission, how are you? We were just playing hide-and-seek, you want to play too? Suraya isn't very good and she keeps losing, but I keep telling her she just has to try a bit harder, she isn't really using her imagination lah when it comes to hiding, you know?"

Mama no longer looked irritated, just slightly shell-shocked at this barrage of words. "I'm . . . fine," she said finally. "And it is nice to meet you, of course. But shouldn't you be heading home? It will get dark soon, and your mother may worry. There is a bus back to town in about fifteen minutes; if you hurry, you can make it."

"Oh sure, sure," Jing said. "I'll just get my stuff."

Mama nodded stiffly. "Good. And in the meantime, I will start making our dinner." She turned and swept back down the hall toward the kitchen.

"Phew!" Jing said, making an exaggerated show of wiping sweat off her brow. "That was a close one!"

The marble seemed to grow heavier in Suraya's pocket, and she shifted uncomfortably as they walked back to her room. "That was a close one," she echoed.

"Okay, so we have the address on the letters, which should be the last place your grandmother lived—" Jing squinted at her phone. "Some village near Gua Musang. Sound familiar to you?" She poked her finger at Pink, who jumped out of the way.

Not at all. And get your fingers away from me. Do you never clean beneath your nails?

"He says no." Suraya decided to leave out that last bit.

"Well, it's where we're going." Jing shrugged and turned back to her screen, jabbing away at it intently. "I can get us bus tickets there. Not too expensive. I still have my mom's credit card number from that time she couldn't figure out how to buy shoes online and I had to do it for her before she broke her phone. . . ."

"Won't your mom find out?"

Jing shrugged. "I mean, she'll find everything out eventually. Might as well make sure she has plenty to get angry about."

Suraya took a deep breath and nodded. "Do it. We'll leave tomorrow morning. Dress for school as usual and make a run for it as soon as we're dropped off at the gate."

Jing nodded and turned her attention back to her phone.

Suraya turned to Pink, still staring out of the window. "Do you think this is going to work?" It was only now dawning on her, how she was about to lose Pink forever, how harsh a word *forever* really was. "I need you to say it," she whispered. "I need you to tell me we're doing the right thing. That we have to try."

What choice do we have? His voice was resigned, and a little sad.

Jing came to stand beside her, reaching down to clasp Suraya's hand in hers. "Do or do not," she murmured. "There is no try."

TWENTY-SIX

girl

IN THE END, the hardest part was convincing Mama to let her go to school.

It was dinnertime when she decided to broach the subject, and even then, she ran over five possible conversation starters before she decided on the best one.

"Mama," she began as her mother spooned fried rice into her mouth and grimaced.

"Too salty," Mama said shortly, taking a sip of water.

"Sorry," she said. "So, Mama, I was thinking . . . I'd like to go back to school tomorrow."

Mama turned sharp eyes on her, peering closely as if trying to see what was going on inside Suraya's brain. "Is that really wise? Are you . . . well?" Mama never referred to Pink if she could help it; she only talked in roundabout ways about Suraya's "episodes," as if she were a TV series with neatly portioned out doses of drama, easy enough to endure as long as her issues only lasted sixty minutes or less.

"I'm feeling much better," Suraya said, trying to infuse her voice with as much enthusiasm as she could. "I mean, I've been home for a few days now, and you know, I haven't been hearing or seeing anything . . . different. . . . I think the rest really helped. And I miss my friends."

"Hmm." Mama took another mouthful of rice, her face unreadable. Suraya could smell the familiar scent of Tiger Balm wafting gently from where Mama had massaged it into her neck and shoulders to take away the accumulated aches of the day; the potency of it made her sneeze.

"Please, Mama." She shuffled the rice around her plate, making patterns out of carrot cubes and chicken slivers. "I think it would be good for me. Honestly."

It seemed to take years, but finally her mother let out a heavy sigh. "All right. But the minute anything strange starts to happen, anything at all, you're coming straight home and I'm calling the pawang there and then, full moon or no full moon. Got it?"

Suraya felt her heart constrict at the mention of the pawang. "Got it," she said, and they ate the rest of their meal in familiar, uncomfortable silence.

～

Jing's face when they met in front of the school the next morning was alive with exactly the kind of barely suppressed excitement you might expect from someone about to do something she isn't supposed to do. "Oh my gooooood, I can't believe we're doing this!" Her squeal was so loud several girls turned to look at them.

"Shut up, Jing," Suraya hissed, trying her best to look nonchalant. "Everyone's going to know we're ditching."

In her shirt pocket, Pink sighed and rolled his eyes. *You will be caught before you even make it five steps away from the school gate at this rate.*

"*You* shut up," Jing whispered to Suraya, her face indignant. "I can be stealthy, okay? Like a spy, or like . . . like . . . Leia disguised as a bounty hunter to save Han."

She is speaking in tongues again.

"If we're going to make it through today, you guys really have to try and get along," Suraya told him sternly.

"Get along?" Jing shot Pink a suspicious look. "Did he say something about me? What was it? Was it rude? I bet it was rude."

Suraya ignored her and glanced at the gate, where dozens of girls in varying states of sleepiness were milling through to the hall, waiting for the school bell to ring. "Come on, let's go."

They began walking briskly in the other direction, heading

for the shops across the street. "Walk with purpose," Suraya said to Jing under her breath. "If anyone asks, we're just going to go buy some buns because you forgot your lunch."

"Okay, okay, ya, I know," Jing whispered back. Together they walked, step by step by step, and the farther away they got from the school, the more Suraya felt her stomach tighten, expecting to be caught at any moment.

Instead of heading for the sundry shop, where brightly colored bouncy bells in net bags hung suspended from hooks over the entryway and all sorts of sweets clothed in lurid packaging were displayed in a way calculated to tempt even the most levelheaded child into parting with her pocket money, they slipped into the little-used alleyway behind the shophouses and pressed their bodies close against the wall, just as the school bell rang in the distance.

It was the custom for prefects to be stationed at the gate during assembly, keeping a sharp lookout for fugitives and stragglers. Pink hopped onto the worn handlebars of a nearby motorcycle and kept up a steady stream of updates. *There is a tall one with metal on her teeth; long, straight hair; and a way of looking at everyone else as if they were worms,* he supplied.

"Farah," Jing whispered. "She's a form 4 prefect, remember? She modeled one time for an Insta shop that sells fake handbags imported from China or wherever, and ever since she's called herself a model. Carries around a Chanel wallet that she says is real." Jing snorted. "Someone should tell her *Chanel* isn't spelled with two *l*'s."

"Shhh," Suraya hissed, looking around nervously. Jing had a tendency to raise her voice when she got excited. "Who's the other one, Pink?"

The other girl is stout and has shoulder-length hair that she wears swept into combs on either side of her head, and a mole at the corner of her mouth. He paused to listen before continuing. *She seems to take great delight in barking out orders to smaller students who have the misfortune of being late.*

The two girls exchanged looks. "Bulldog," they whispered at exactly the same time. Bulldog's real name was Maria; she was sixteen and believed that if she enforced the school rules to the letter, she'd have a real shot at being head girl when she was seventeen. Being head girl was the dream of Bulldog's heart, and she threw herself into her prefectorial duties with all the enthusiasm and ferocity of the animal that was her nickname. Being caught by Bulldog, they knew, would mean a brisk march to the principal's office and the end of their mission.

"Can't let her catch us," Jing said softly, looking as worried as Suraya felt. Suraya nodded.

And then Jing's phone rang.

The tinny notes of the Imperial March blared through the quiet morning air like a foghorn. "Stop it, quickly, turn it off!" Suraya hissed as Jing's eyes widened in panic, and she fumbled to get her phone out of her pocket. "Why do you even have it with you?! That's against school rules!"

"YOU try telling my mother she can't contact me during the day! Want me to die is it?"

The stout one is looking this way, Pink said warningly.

"Jing, TURN OFF YOUR PHONE." If a whisper could also be a shout, Suraya's was a bellow. In her confusion, Jing accidentally pressed the green Answer Call button, and her mother's shrill voice wafted through the receiver. "Ah girl? Can you hear me? You forgot your lunch lah, you need me to bring to you? Hello? Hello?"

"Jing!" Suraya's voice was imploring.

Jing finally managed to locate the button that powered her phone down and Aunty Soo's voice fizzled into silence.

They waited, holding their breath.

They are conferring, Pink said. *They keep looking over here with puzzled expressions. The tall one is saying, "But there is nobody there."*

A pause. Then Pink: *The stout one is walking this way.*

Oh no. "Bulldog's coming," Suraya whispered, and Jing shot her a look of pure despair. Suraya cast around desperately, looking for somewhere they could hide. But except for the wrappers and cigarette butts scattered carelessly along the alleyway, there was nowhere to go. Instead, she pressed her body as close to the wall as it would go and prayed for Bulldog to lose interest and go away.

She is getting closer.

They could hear her now, walking toward where they stood hidden. Bulldog's steps were distinctive; she didn't walk so much as march everywhere she went, the steady thud of her footsteps announcing her arrival well before you actually saw her face.

"Maria!" It was the high-pitched voice of their discipline teacher Mrs. Ng, laced with a generous dose of irritation. "Maria! What ARE you doing?"

"I heard something just now, teacher!" Bulldog yelled back. "I just wanted to check it out."

"Nonsense! There's nothing there but rubbish and bad smells." The teacher's sniff carried all the way to where the two girls stood, their hearts pounding, Bulldog just steps away. "Get back here at once. Assembly is over, and classes are about to begin."

"Okay, teacher." The reply was grumpy, but Suraya knew Bulldog would do as she was told. The rules were too important to ignore.

Sure enough, the heavy steps thudded back toward the school, getting fainter and fainter until they couldn't be heard at all.

They are gone, Pink said at last. *It is safe for you to come out now.*

They changed in a scrub of woodland by the shophouses, fishing their regular clothes out of the bottoms of their backpacks and taking turns, careful not to glance at each other's bodies for fear of embarrassing each other (and themselves). Jing had turned her phone back on as soon as the coast was clear, and it took Suraya fifteen painful minutes to stop her friend agonizing over how to respond to her mother("I HUNG UP on her, Sooz, she's going to KILL ME") and put on the baju kurung Suraya had brought for her from home and insisted she wear. Jing was fine with this; what she wasn't fine with was the fact that nothing about it fit the way it was supposed to.

"These sleeves are too long," Jing moaned, waving her hands so that the excess material flapped about. "The waist is too big. The sarong is dragging on the floor. I feel like a little kid playing dress-up."

"Stop complaining lah." Suraya reached over and began to fold Jing's sleeves. "Look, see? We fold this up, then we fold at the waist, it'll be fine. We want people to believe we're sisters, right? And anyway, it's a sign of respect."

Jing frowned. "Respect of what? A sign to who?"

"When we visit a cemetery. It's a sign of respect to the dead to be dressed modestly. Right, Pink?"

The ghost shrugged. *I do not know. It sounds like a very human rule to me.*

Suraya looked at him. "Really?" It was a thing she'd been told almost her entire life, and it unmoored her slightly to hear that it didn't really seem to matter to a ghost himself.

The dead don't really think about what you're wearing, he said matter-of-factly. *Mostly on account of being dead.*

"Well, whatever the ghost thinks, I don't have any other clothes, so unless the dead are okay with me being naked, this is what we're going with," said Jing.

The dead definitely do not want that.

"I'm not sure the living want that either," said Suraya.

Jing sighed noisily. "I may not be able to HEAR him, but I KNOW when you two are making fun of me, okay?!"

They walked to the bus station in town, keeping close to walls and shadows when they could and trying to be as inconspicuous as possible.

Inside, the little building was stifling; the walls bore flaking off-white paint, travel posters peeling at the corners, and an aging air-conditioning unit that groaned and belched out stale gusts of air every couple of minutes. Jing had booked their seats online, so all they had to do was find the right counter and collect their tickets. Still, they couldn't risk getting sloppy, not when they were so close.

"Let me do the talking," Suraya said, shifting her backpack so that it sat more evenly on her shoulders. Jing still had the highly excitable look of exactly what she was: a kid skipping school.

"Okay," she said agreeably.

They walked up to the counter, where a bored-looking woman in a pink headscarf tapped away at a game on her phone. Technicolor shapes beeped and booped and erupted in explosions of rainbow pixels as Suraya stood and waited to be acknowledged.

"Excuse m—"

"Wait ah." The woman held up one finger, her eyes still glued to her screen, her thumb moving rapidly.

"Umm. Okay." They shuffled their feet awkwardly and waited. Every minute that dragged by, Suraya's stomach knotted itself even further, until she thought she might throw up from sheer anxiety.

More beeps and boops and one final explosion later, the woman sighed and put her phone down. "Can I help you?" she asked. The tone of her voice implied that she was doing them a huge favor by asking.

"Umm, we booked tickets online?"

"Booking number," the woman said gruffly. "Please," she added as an afterthought.

Jing fished her phone out of her pocket, and Suraya quickly read off the string of letters and numbers as the woman entered them into her computer.

"Two tickets to Gua Musang, Kelantan?" she asked.

"Yeah."

"Hold on." More tapping, and then the steady screech of an ancient printer. The woman's eyes finally flicked over the two of them, and she frowned slightly. "A little young to be traveling so far all by yourselves, aren't you? No school today?"

Suraya froze. Beside her, she saw Jing's arm move. "These are not the droids you're looking for," Jing mumbled, and Suraya quickly kicked her in the shin. "Ow!"

Suraya fixed her most winning smile on the woman with the pink headscarf. "Our grandmother is sick, and our mom left us with our dad and went to take care of her," she said, her mind racing. "But now, uh . . . Opah is REALLY sick— like, dying and stuff—and our dad can't take time off, but she really wants to see us, so . . ." She trailed off.

Jing let out a theatrical sob. "Poor Opah."

The woman had already lost interest. "Whatever. Here you go. Platform 2." She slid the tickets across the counter and Suraya grabbed them eagerly. "Just be careful. Don't talk to strangers," she added as an afterthought.

"We won't. Thank you!" They scampered away as quickly as they could, before she could ask them any more questions.

Not that they needed to worry. *She is playing her game again,* Pink observed once they were a safe distance away. *And she is losing. She is not very good.*

"I wonder if I should have told her the cheat code for that level," Jing mused at almost exactly the same time. "Because she really sucked at that game, man. Oh well. Come on, let's go find platform 2 before she thinks of more questions to ask us."

In their hurry to get away from the disinterested ticket lady, they didn't notice the plump figure of a man just a few steps away.

On a bench in a corner near the dustbins was the pawang, watching them intently.

TWENTY-SEVEN

ghost

A RANDOM TUESDAY morning, as it turned out, was an excellent day for covert missions involving bus travel, because aside from an impeccably dressed gray-haired couple holding hands and a polished wooden cane each, a young man with headphones that sat atop an impossibly shaggy head of hair, and three girls in headscarves who went to sleep as soon as they settled into their seats, they had the entire bus to themselves.

According to Jing's phone, the journey to Gua Musang was supposed to take about four hours. But that was if they didn't make any stops along the way. And as it turned out, this was a bus that did stop along the way, meandering into little towns and villages to load and offload passengers.

The girls has been optimistic about this at first, using the time to go over the plan again and again and again. "We'll go to the graveyard and look for a little kid's grave," Jing would say. "And then when we figure out which one is Pink's, we'll dig a hole for him there," Suraya would continue, "so he can rejoin his body."

The rest of me. Pink repeated the words softly to himself, remembering the smell of damp earth and decaying flesh, the feel of living things wriggling all around him in the darkness. How to explain this feeling in the pit of his stomach? How to tell the only person he cared for that the rest of him was her, and not some pile of bones deep underground? Not for the first time, Pink cursed the emotions he was trying so hard not to feel. *That's what you get, being around them for so long,* he thought dourly. *Humanity is contagious.*

But he bit back his bitter thoughts as he watched the two go over and over their plan, and said nothing, not even as he saw their enthusiasm slowly begin to dip lower and lower with each stop the bus made, until it wheezed to a halt so their fearsomely mustached driver could have his lunch.

"This is going to take forever," Suraya said in despair. It was already 12:17 p.m.; they'd left at 9:27 when they were supposed to leave at 9:00 a.m.—a delay that was never explained—and they'd been here for an hour already, sitting on a bench spotted with peeling paint and rust spots and waiting for the driver, who was now taking luxuriant drags of a cigarette as he loudly talked politics with other taxi and bus drivers at the warong nearby. He was so relaxed that Pink was seriously considering a well-placed hex that would make his entire mustache fall in clumps into his gently sweating glass of iced lemon tea.

Their destination was still almost an hour away, and there were countless stops before they got there. Suraya couldn't stop moving, whether it was a jiggling leg or a tapping finger, and Pink could tell she was just about ready to crawl out of her own skin. He couldn't blame her—he was starting to feel the same way himself.

"Relax lah," Jing said, taking a swig from a water bottle festooned with tiny Wookiees. "We have time."

I wouldn't be so sure if I were her. It is only a matter of time before someone realizes you are gone, Pink pointed out.

"I doubt anyone will notice when it comes to me," Suraya muttered darkly. "Pink says people are going to notice we're gone soon," she said in answer to Jing's confused expression.

"But it's not like they know where we went," Jing said reasonably. "And even when we get there, it's not like we can do anything until, like, really late at night. Imagine what all the old mosque uncles will say if they see two little girls digging up a grave in the middle of the afternoon."

Suraya laughed in spite of herself. "You have a point." She smiled and grabbed Jing's hand. "I'm really glad you're here."

"Me too, Sooz."

Pink sat on her shoulder, trying not to mind how easy they were with each other, how comfortable. How right. It was hard to look at them and not ask himself: *Were we ever that way together?*

"You okay, Pink?" Suraya nudged him gently with one finger.

He stirred. *I am as well as can be expected,* he said.

"Are you excited to be heading home?" They watched as Jing wiped the sweat from her forehead with a tissue, then crumpled it into a ball and tossed it into a nearby trash can. It missed, landing softly on the floor, and she clicked her tongue in irritation as she got up to retrieve it.

No, Pink said. *It was not a home. I just occupied space there.*

"Was my grandmother not nice to you, Pink?"

He thought about this for a long time, trying to ignore the tears in Suraya's eyes. *This witch was not really very nice to anyone,* he said slowly. *But I suppose she was nicer to me than to most others, because I was useful to her.*

"She doesn't sound like someone I would have liked."

Most people did not like the witch, and she did not care about being liked. Some people are like that. He nuzzled her cheek softly, trying to take the sting out of his words. *Not you. Never you. But some people.*

Across the street, their bus driver stood up, his red plastic stool scraping harshly across the concrete floor of the warong. They watched as he hitched up his pants and bid his fellow drivers goodbye.

"Back on the road," Jing said, and they clambered back onto the bus once again.

It was just after 4:00 p.m. by the time the old blue bus sputtered into the little village just outside Gua Musang, where Suraya got the driver to drop them off on his way to the big town. Jing and Suraya got off and tried to stretch the stiffness from their limbs as the bus roared away. Suraya's shoulder sported a dark patch where she'd drooled in her sleep, and Pink saw her quickly pull her hair forward to cover it, hoping nobody would notice. Jing definitely hadn't; she was too busy rubbing her rear, a look of consternation on her face. "It's totally NUMB, Sooz," she said, craning her head to look at it. "Like I can't feel it AT ALL."

Please tell your friend to stop yelling about her buttocks,

Pink said drily. *We are trying to be incognito, after all.*

"Shh, Jing, people are looking."

"No they're not," Jing shot back, still grimacing, hands on her rear. "There's too much going on for them to notice."

And it was true. The bus had deposited them in the middle of a bustling scene, near a market from which came the over-powering smell of fresh fish guts and wet garbage.

"I didn't think it would be . . . like this," Suraya said. "Where did all these people come from? Where do we go now?" Pink had to hang on for dear life to her shoulder; as Suraya spoke, she dodged a motorcycle that whizzed by, then quickly ducked out of the way as a plump older lady strode past them, one hand holding a wicker basket filled to the brim with spoils from the market, the other hanging on to a little boy no older than five or six. He dragged his feet as he walked, kicking at pebbles, his mouth twisted into a mutinous pout. When he saw them watching, he stuck out his tongue and pulled the most grotesque face before his mother pulled him away, scolding as she went.

Jing fished her phone out of her pocket and plugged the address into a navigation app. "This way," she said, pointing. There was a bright little ding.

"Another message from your mom?" Suraya asked.

"Uh-huh." Jing's mother had begun sending more and more texts once 2:00 p.m. passed and she still wasn't home, and after a while Jing had just stopped responding.

Where r u

i bought u McDonalds for lunch

did u forget to tell me u have extra class or somethg

The latest one she showed Suraya just said **CALL ME** in all caps, with a period at the end.

"She used punctuation." Jing gulped. "That can't be good."

Suraya laid a comforting hand on her friend's shoulder. Then, because they had to keep going, they started walking.

"What. Is. Going. On."

Where the witch's house was supposed to be was no house at all. Instead it was an upmarket café, complete with an extensive menu of specialty coffee written in an overly fancy font on a massive chalkboard, an interior replete with wood and chrome and exposed brick, and hipsters in tight jeans and horn-rimmed glasses.

Pink turned accusingly to Jing, who shrugged helplessly. *Do we have the right address?*

"Do we have the right address, Jing?" Suraya repeated.

"Ya, of course!" Stung, Jing shoved her own glasses so they

sat more firmly on her nose and stuck her phone in Suraya's face. "See, Sooz? Tell him. No mistakes."

"I don't understand," Suraya whispered.

I do, Pink said grimly. *It came.*

"It?" Suraya asked. Jing was peering at them curiously now, trying to figure out what was going on.

Progress. The word tasted bitter on his tongue. The witch had always been worried about progress, modernization slowly leeching away whatever belief people had left in the old ways and the old ghosts, "rendering old beings like you and I utterly useless," she'd tell him with an indignant sniff.

And so here it was, their demise, in the form of overpriced coffee, free Wi-Fi, and too-loud folk covers of tepid pop songs.

"What do we do now?" Suraya wondered.

"Get a coffee?" They both turned to stare at Jing, and she shrugged. "What? Does anyone else have any bright ideas?"

They didn't.

They sat at a round table by the glass walls that faced the main road, on hard wooden stools that were high on aesthetic value and low on comfort. Suraya ordered a bottle of expensive French mineral water because they didn't serve the regular kind. Jing ordered a cappuccino because "it sounds damn sophisticated," then began spluttering as soon as she had her first sip.

"Why do people drink coffee?!" she whimpered, taking a swig from Suraya's bottle. "This tastes terrible."

I believe they call it an acquired taste, Pink said drily. *Much like yourself.*

Suraya smirked in spite of herself. "Pink! Behave."

"IS HE TALKING ABOUT ME AGAIN??" Jing made a big show of taking a deep breath and pointedly ignoring Pink. From a pocket came another urgent ding. "So what should we do now?"

Suraya sighed as she reached up to retie her ponytail. "We could try the cemetery I guess? See if there's anything we can figure out from there. It's a body we're looking for, after all."

"True also. We—"

It was at this exact moment, before Jing had even finished her sentence, that Pink glanced outside.

And froze.

Across the street stood the pawang. He was perfectly still, save for the cloth of his voluminous robe, which flapped restlessly in the breeze created by the cars that zipped past. He was staring straight at them, the late afternoon sun glinting off his glasses. And as Pink watched, he smiled a slow, chilling smile.

Without even thinking, without missing a beat, Pink waved his antennae.

Nothing happened at first. At least, not until Jing, staring down at her still-full cup with distaste, said, "What . . . is that?"

Then the screams began.

Out of every crack, every crevice, every shadowy nook, the cockroaches came. They poured out onto every available surface, they swam in mugs of lukewarm coffee, they popped out of the creamy centers of fluffy pastries, and one enterprising bug even managed to crawl out from beneath the folds of one young lady's intricately wrapped hijab.

The back door, Pink said quickly into Suraya's ear. *And quickly.* As he surveyed the chaos all around them, it was hard not to feel a twinge of guilt for causing it—the lady with the hijab in particular seemed extremely displeased, to put it mildly. But he had no choice. Because when Pink looked at the pawang again, right on the brink of sending swarms of bees to hound him, he suddenly realized that he recognized the look on the pawang's face.

It was glee.

It dawned on Pink right then and there that the pawang was *enjoying* this. It was nothing more than a game to him, and Pink himself was the prize to be won. And then Pink remembered the rows and rows of ghosts and spirits, with their malevolent stares and their restless movements, and he looked at the two girls and the throngs of hipsters and thought: *I cannot let him unleash his monsters here.*

Chaos was the only other option.

As the two girls pushed their way through the throng of shrieking patrons and the one bearded employee who was trying to smash cockroaches with a jar of Honduran coffee beans, Pink looked back over his shoulder.

But where the pawang had stood, there was nothing but air and shadows.

girl

OUTSIDE, BEHIND THE coffee shop, Suraya and Jing paused to catch their breath. Jing wore an expression of sheer disgust. "Ohmygod, Sooz, do you think I drank it? Is that why it tasted so bad? What if I just drank, like, cockroach juice coffee?" Her face took on a distinctly gray shade.

Tell your friend to relax, Pink said, peering up and down the tiny alleyway that stretched on beyond the back door. *We are alone now.* As if to prove him wrong, a lone cockroach skittered past, making soft clicking sounds against the cement floor, and causing Jing to jump as though her toes were on fire.

. . . except for that one, he acknowledged.

"That was . . . odd," Suraya said slowly, and though she looked straight at Pink as she said it, she noticed he was very careful not to meet her eye.

He made a great show of shrugging his little grasshopper shoulders. *The only odd thing was how they ever passed a health inspection with an infestation like that.*

"Did you have anything to do with that?" She hated to ask, mostly because she had the nagging feeling that she knew exactly what the answer would be, and wouldn't like it at all. And maybe Pink knew that too, because all he did was look away.

"I need a shower," Jing muttered, rubbing her arms as if she could still feel the march of tiny cockroach legs on her skin. "Or two showers. Fifteen, even." *Ding,* went Jing's phone. "Stop it, Ma," she muttered to herself.

"No time for that," Suraya told her. "We've got a cemetery to visit."

And a body to find.

Jing wrinkled her nose. "Okay, then, captain. Lead the way."

Tucked away from the crowded town center, the cemetery was trim and neat, the grass free of weeds, the head- and tail stones of each grave scrubbed clean.

Suraya had thought she would be a little afraid of it, even in broad daylight. There was something about the idea of knowing bodies were hidden in the ground beneath your feet that intimidated her. Yet there was nothing scary about this place or its bodies. It was too clean, too organized, too arranged, like the sterile, fluorescent-lit aisles of a supermarket.

"So . . . how do we even do this?" Jing asked, scratching her nose.

"I don't know," Suraya said. "But we know we're looking for a small grave. It's a start."

"Not much of a start."

"It's all we've got," Suraya pointed out. Her head was starting to hurt. "Let's split up. You too, Pink."

He hadn't expected that; she could tell from the way his little body stiffened, almost imperceptibly. But she needed, more than anything right now, to be alone.

As you wish.

He bounded off her shoulder, and the three began to move in different directions in the narrow spaces between stones.

Remember, Pink called out. *Look for children. That will limit your search somewhat.*

Suraya repeated the words for Jing, who nodded but said nothing in reply.

For a long time, the only sound in the cemetery was the

faint whistling of the wind whirling through the trees that shaded the graves.

The sun was bright, and Suraya's eyes soon grew tired from trying to make out the names on each headstone, some spelled out entirely in the curving Arabic script that she had to work harder to recognize. She paused beneath the spreading boughs of a tree so gnarled with age that she couldn't even tell what fruit it might have once borne, and wiped the sweat off her brow. Then she reached into her pocket, where the marble lay snug in its cloth trappings. She wanted to feel the smoothness of its surface, the reassuring weight of it in her hand. She wanted to be comforted by its gentle, oddly familiar warmth.

But not this time.

As she reached down to brush it with her fingers, she felt it—a sharp bite of electricity that made her squeal.

She stared at her hand in confusion. Get a grip, Suraya, she told herself firmly. It's just a marble. Steeling herself, she reached into her pocket again.

This time her agonized yelp echoed across the cemetery, bouncing off the stones until it reached Jing and Pink, who turned to her with puzzled faces.

"You okay, Sooz?" Jing called.

"Fine," she called back. "Just . . . uh, tripped."

Be careful, Pink told her.

"Stop nagging," she muttered under her breath. Gritting her teeth, she plunged her hand into her pocket and grabbed the marble firmly, ignoring the shot of current that immediately jolted through it and buzzed in her ears.

The marble was vibrating.

"What in the world . . ." Suraya tried to remember to breathe, but she couldn't seem to get it right. For a fleeting instant, she considered throwing the marble as far away from her as she could, gathering up her friends, and going home.

Then she remembered the pawang, and all that was at stake here.

She stared at the quivering orb resting in the palm of her hand. "Okay, then," she whispered. "You wanted my attention. Now you've got it. What do you want? What do I do with you?"

She half-expected a voice to answer from within its glassy depths, but there was only silence.

Feeling slightly foolish, she held it to her ear, listening for instructions that never came. Then she surreptitiously rubbed it with her fingers, the way Aladdin rubbed the lamp, in case there was even the slightest chance a genie would appear.

None did.

In despair, she held the marble up to her eye, trying to see if there was a message she might have missed within.

Instead, as if she was looking right through it, she saw a tall, thin figure sitting in the tree. He had a gaunt, pale face and dark, mournful eyes that were trained directly at her.

The thing opened its mouth.

"You sweat a lot," it said.

Suraya blinked. Then she blinked again. She took the marble away from her eye, and the being in the tree disappeared. She put it back, and there he was again. He was clearly there, even if he wasn't entirely solid; she could see straight through his body to the pits and grooves and contours of the branch he sat on.

"Don't talk much, do you?" The ghost, as it was becoming obvious to her this thing was, regarded her closely. She could just make out the faint outline of the plain T-shirt and loose black pants he wore, the oval shape of the black songkok perched on his shaggy head. He looked like he was in his early twenties and somehow also as if he had been around for a very, very long time. "I'd expected more from the likes of you."

"The likes of me?"

"Witch, aren't you?" He bent down to peer at her. "You've

got a clearly enchanted object there. Bit young, though." He straightened up again. "Ooh, or is this a quest? It's a quest, isn't it? That's how it is with these things. You've got a magical object, you've got either someone clever with witchery, or you've got someone on some sort of hero's journey. That's how it always was in the books." He peered at her again. "You don't look much like a hero, to be sure."

"Why not?"

"You're a girl, for one thing."

This was the last straw. She had not come all this way to be insulted by someone who was already dead. "How would you know what a hero looks like anyway? If you can spew nonsense like that, my guess is you didn't interact with too many girls while you were alive. . . ."

The ghost bristled at this. "Insolent little thing," he sniffed. "When I was alive, the likes of you would have been taken to task for such impertinence."

"I'm sorry." She shrugged. "But you're not. Alive, that is. And you started it, you know."

The ghost pouted. "I was only playing," he said sullenly. "You needn't have been so hurtful. One can't help contracting bloody dengue fever, after all."

"It's true," she said consolingly. "You couldn't very well

have stopped it once you had it." She thought of the campaigns her school had run to help prevent the spread of dengue, then thought better of mentioning them. Nobody wants to know the ways you can avoid your own death—at least, not when you're already dead.

The ghost sighed. "Ah well. Why dwell on the past, eh?" He stuck out a hand, before realizing what he'd done and putting it into his pocket with a sheepish expression. "Name's Hussein."

"Suraya."

"Well, then, Miss Suraya, what brings you to our neck of the woods?" Hussein gestured expansively around the cemetery.

"Our?" Suraya glanced up and down the headstones; there was no other ghost in sight. "You seem to be the only one out and about."

Hussein shrugged. "The others don't see much point in hanging about during the day," he said. "They sleep. Even at night, there's not much of a social life in these parts. Once in a while, there's a mixer, during the full moon. That's about it." He sighed again. "Lot of old folks here. Dead boring, it is. Oh hey, that's a pun!" He laughed aloud, delighted with himself, as Suraya smiled dutifully.

"How about children?" she asked, trying hard to keep her

voice light, casual, as if the answer wasn't a matter of life and death. "Any children here?"

Hussein frowned. "Not too many," he said. "It's a thriving little town, see. Infant mortality isn't too much of an issue here. You've got one or two babies—stillbirths, the saddest little things, the older aunties do love having them to cuddle, though—a couple of drownings, one car crash . . ."

"Can you take me to see them?"

"Um, Sooz?" As if by magic, Jing materialized at her side, her expression wary. "You do realize you're talking to yourself, right?"

"I hate to break it to you, Jing," Suraya said, passing her the marble, as Pink bounded onto her shoulder. "But . . . I'm really not."

There was a muffled gasp, then a breathless, "Cooooooooooooooooool."

I see we have found ourselves some company.

"You can see him?"

Pink shrugged a grasshopper shrug. *We are of the same kind.*

"Like family."

On very remote branches of the same tree.

"So what do you miss most?" Jing said, addressing the tree branch very seriously. "Nasi lemak or roti canai?"

Suraya snatched back the marble, ignoring Jing's protests. "Hussein, can you take us to see the children's graves?"

"Of course." In one smooth leap, the ghost jumped down from the tree and dusted some nonexistent debris from his noncorporeal rear. "Follow me, ladies. And for the record," he said over his shoulder, "the answer is nasi lemak. With a side of crispy fried chicken. Mmm."

There were three graves. They were small.

The four of them stood and stared at the names—Intan, aged four; Ahmad, aged two; Liyana, aged two.

Is this all? Pink said.

"Not many kiddies here, like I said," said Hussein, in almost apologetic tones. "There might be a few more, I can check . . ." He scratched his ghostly head. "Why do you even want to see them, though? I won't lie to you, it's more than a mite depressing sometimes, seeing the little ones."

"We have our reasons. Can you . . . can you call the children?" Suraya's palms were sweaty, and the marble felt slick and precarious in her grasp.

Hussein snapped off a smart salute. "As you wish, m'lady."

He went to the first grave (Liyana, aged two) and rapped on the headstone. "Assalamualaikum, little sister. Wake up, we have visitors."

At first all was still, and Jing jabbed Suraya in the waist surreptitiously. "Is something supposed to happen ah?"

It was a good thing Suraya held the marble, because Hussein's glare was so icy it would have given Jing frostbite.

"Patience," he said stiffly. "Sabar. I mean, have you ever tried waking up a two-year-old? I think not." He turned back to the headstone and rapped again—a little harder this time. "Wake up, little sister."

If you were looking, you might have noticed the earth move, ever so slightly, right at the foot of the grave.

Then, slowly, a figure began to glide out of the ground, a figure through which Suraya could see the outlines of the cemetery's rows and rows of head- and tail stones.

The little girl ghost rubbed her eyes, glared at Hussein and said, "WHAT?"

She can speak, Pink said quietly. *She has her tongue.*

"She's not the one." Suraya's heart sank. "She's not the one we're looking for."

The little girl glared up at her. "Then why you wake me UP?" Without another word, she flounced off and sank back into the earth where she'd emerged from.

"That went well," Hussein said, smiling brightly. "Next one?"

They tried them all, one after the other: Intan, aged four.

Ahmad, aged two. They tried Khairul, aged six, hidden in a shadowy corner Hussein had forgotten about. They even tried Melati, aged eight, and Mariam, aged twelve, who rolled her eyes impressively when asked about her tongue and stuck it out to show them before disappearing (although not before telling Jing "Your glasses are dorky.")

"This is hopeless," Jing said crossly, pushing her glasses more firmly up her nose. "And my glasses ARE NOT DORKY," she added, yelling at the ground for good measure, as if Mariam could hear her.

"What do we do now, Pink?" Suraya asked quietly.

I . . . I do not know.

"What happened to the wisdom of the ages, huh?" She tried to laugh, but it came out limp and weak, and Pink didn't even smile in response.

Behind them, Jing was still casting dark looks at the spot where Mariam had been. "What does she know, anyway," she muttered.

"You'll have to forgive Mariam," Hussein said cheerily. "She's always grumpy. Doesn't get many visitors, you know. The family was living here when she died, but then everyone moved away. Too many painful memories and all that. They only come to visit every few months or so. Tough when you don't live where your dear ones lay buried. . . ."

"That's it," Suraya said suddenly.

Everyone turned to look at her.

"Where you die isn't necessarily where you lived," she said. "The witch—my grandmother—you said she moved a lot, right? We just need to figure out where she lived before."

"That's well and good, but how are we going to do that?" Jing gestured to her still-pinging phone. "We haven't exactly got a ton of time. And it's starting to get dark."

Suraya felt her spirits dip as low as the sun in the sky.

TWENTY-NINE

ghost

THEY SAT ON the curb in a row outside the cemetery, first the ghostly form of Hussein, then Jing, Suraya, and Pink each casting three long, thin shadows in the waning sunlight.

The ghost cleared his throat awkwardly. "So, um. I have no idea what kind of weird scavenger hunt you girls were on, but this was really fun."

"This was fun for you?" Jing scratched absentmindedly at the border of where skin met cast, and Suraya nudged to make her stop.

"I mean. I don't, uh, get many visitors myself."

"Why not?" Suraya's voice was gentle, and Pink knew how badly she wanted to keep Hussein from hurting. If there was anything he knew from his time with Suraya, it was that she could never bear anyone to feel pain, not even the bullies who had plagued her for so long.

Pink could see the ghost shrug, trying to put on a cloak of bravado he clearly didn't feel. "They stopped coming one year, my parents. It's been a long, long time. My guess is they died, and now they're buried somewhere else. Somewhere far away from me."

Pink's nonexistent heart broke slightly for this ghost, who ached for a family long gone, and for himself too, though he would never admit it. In her own way, the witch had been family—she had created him, after all, and for a long time she was all he had known. He wished he could say he cared for her more than he did.

There was silence.

Then Suraya spoke. "I will come back, you know. To see you. I will."

Hussein smiled. "I'd like that very much." He sighed. "It wouldn't be so bad if I wasn't having so much trouble remembering their faces. I remember them in fragments: the smell of my father's cigars, the pattern on his favorite sarong. The way my mother's hands felt on my face when she put talcum powder on me before school, the songs she'd sing while cooking in the kitchen. But I can't for the life of me remember their faces." He pushed back a handful of ghostly hair. "If only I had a picture or something."

A picture.

The little girl with the lopsided pictures and the lopsided smile.

The letters, pleading at first, and then suddenly cold. *Do not contact us again.*

Pink stiffened. *I remember.*

Suraya looked at him. "Remember what, Pink?"

"What?" Jing was suddenly alert. "What does he remember?"

The village. The place I was born . . . made. He frowned, trying his hardest to pull it from his memories, turn fragments into something whole, solid, usable. Jambu trees in the garden. A round pond. A blue-domed mosque. And something else. Something about where they lived that always made the witch say . . .

Elephants never forget, he said.

"What?"

Something the witch used to say. It was one of his earliest memories. Light filtering through damp, dark earth, and the witch's face, creased with smiles and wet with tears. *Elephants never forget, and I never want to forget you,* she'd crooned.

"Is anyone else confused?" Jing asked. "Or is it just me?"

The witch lived in a village with elephants in its name. Gajah.

Suraya relayed this information to Jing, who pulled out her phone, still dinging incessantly. "That . . . narrows it down a

little bit, but not by much. You'd be surprised how many kam-
pungs in Malaysia have *gajah* in the name."

"Try Perak, Jing," Suraya said. She looked at Pink.
"Remember what Mama said before? To the pawang, that
time? He asked her about the biscuits, her favorite ones. She
said she grew up eating them."

A Perak specialty, he called them. I remember.

Jing jabbed furiously at the screen. "Which one, you think?
Batu Gajah or Kampung Kuala Gajah?"

"Which one has a mosque with a blue dome?"

There was a pause.

"Kampung Kuala Gajah," Hussein said softly.

Pink, Suraya, and Jing exchanged glances. "How do you
know?" Jing said, frowning.

"I went there once." The ghost shrugged. "We were on the
way back to our kampung for Hari Raya—you know, Aidil-
fitri with the grandparents and all. My dad likes . . . liked . . .
to stop at small villages we'd never been before when we were
on long trips like that. Made it like an adventure, you know?"
He paused to clear his throat. "There was a great warong near
the mosque. Trays and trays of dishes, all still fresh and steaming. Masak lemak pucuk ubi and sambal bilis petai and ikan
keli bakar and this huge spread of fresh ulam with the most
amazing sambal belacan." Hussein smiled at the memory.

"Anyway, I remember eating and panting a bit because the sambal belacan was proper spicy, and looking up to see that blue dome shining in the sun. We went there when we were done, to pray Zohor."

He stopped and sighed, staring up at the painted sky. "I miss my parents. I miss food, too."

"No kidding." Jing rubbed her stomach, which was making strange noises. "That story made me hungry. And also made me miss my mom. Just a teensy bit."

And it was at precisely that moment that Jing's phone began to beep incessantly, like a fire alarm. Hussein's eyes widened. "What is happening?"

"It's my phone." Jing wore a puzzled expression.

"That is a PHONE?" Hussein's mouth hung open in wonder. "It's TINY!"

The noise was starting to make Pink's head hurt. *Make it stop that infernal noise.*

"Jing," Suraya spoke through gritted teeth. "What is happening?"

"I don't know. What's . . . oh." In the light of the screen, Pink saw her face grow pale.

"What is it?"

Jing held up the phone for them to see.

At first, Pink couldn't figure out what he was looking at. It looked like a map, the type that reduces buildings and roads to lines and squares. A bright red circle glowed in the center of the map, and the words LOCATING PHONE scrolled over and over again on top of it in a never-ending loop.

Suraya's eyes widened. "Is that . . . ?"

Jing nodded. "She's using the Find My Phone app to locate us."

What does that mean?

"I don't know," Suraya said, her voice shaky with panic. "I don't have a phone, remember? What does that mean, Jing?"

"It means she's using my phone to pinpoint our exact location." She pushed her sweaty hair back off her forehead and grimaced. "Of all the times for my mother to figure out how technology works . . ."

Hussein leaned close to Pink. "Kind of glad to be dead at the moment, really. Kids these days seem to have very stressful lives."

You are not wrong.

There was one final, long beep, and then the phone was silenced.

The two girls looked at each other. Then, slowly, they looked at the screen.

PHONE FOUND.

Jing let out a breath. "They're coming for us."

THIRTY

girl

"WE HAVE TO get to Kampung Kuala Gajah," Suraya said, as they walked briskly back to the town center. "Somehow," she added.

"Okay, but how though?" Jing said, scurrying after her. "And how quickly can we do it, considering our moms may appear, like, at any second?"

"Your mom, maybe." Suraya was still fairly sure her mother had yet to notice she was gone.

This is hyperbole, Pink said. *It would take your mothers at least four hours to arrive at this place, and that is if there were no traffic to hinder them.*

"Pink says you're overreacting."

Jing sighed noisily. "Has he ever heard of dramatic effect?"

Has she ever considered taking five minutes to just . . . not be herself?

"Have you two ever thought about not arguing for once?" Suraya didn't mean to snap, but she was hot and worried and very close to locking the two of them in the cockroach-infested café to work out their differences. "I hate to tell you this, but it is absolutely no fun to be the only person hearing both sides of your bickering. We have too much work to do for this nonsense."

"But how do we do it if we don't know what we're doing?" Jing asked.

It wasn't an unreasonable question, which was what made it so hard to hear.

"First things first." She stared at the phone in Jing's hand, now locked and useless. "Ditch your phone."

"EXCUSE ME?" Jing clutched the phone to her chest, looking appalled. "I can't do that! This is an iPhone!"

Suraya could feel the waves of panic rising higher and higher in her chest. "You have to leave it here, so our mothers don't know to follow us to Perak!"

"So why can't I just SWITCH IT OFF?"

"Does that even work?" She was sweating now.

"Of course it does!" Jing threw her arms up in exasperation. "Don't you know how cell phones work?"

A sudden lump lodged itself in Suraya's throat, and try as she might, she couldn't seem to swallow it away. "You know I don't."

Jing's face was immediately contrite. "Sorry, Sooz. I didn't mean it like that." She sighed and took her glasses off, wiping the smudged lenses on her top. "Look, I just don't think it's a good idea to get rid of my phone. What if there's an emergency?"

Suraya. She felt Pink lay a spindly leg gently on her cheek. *It will be fine. The girl has a point. What if we need the device later on?*

"Fine." Suraya took a deep, wavery breath. "But it stays off the whole time. Got it?"

"Got it."

Ten minutes later, they were walking back toward the center of town.

"Come on," Suraya said over her shoulder as she began to walk toward the bus station. "Let's try and figure out how long it'll take and how much it'll c—oof!" Before she could stop herself, she'd walked straight into the shadowy figure who'd stepped into her path seemingly out of nowhere.

Suraya looked up. It was, she realized, a startlingly familiar shadowy figure.

The pawang.

Suraya's heart lodged itself into her throat.

"Hello, ladies," he said, smiling that too-pleasant smile. "Fancy meeting you here. A little far from home, aren't you?"

The two girls said nothing.

"Do your parents know where you are?" He let his glance drift from Suraya to Jing, then back again, slow, casual, and somehow completely unsettling. He bent down, so close to Suraya's face she could smell the sour staleness of his breath. "I bet you don't want them to."

She stepped back involuntarily, and he smiled that strange, easy smile. "Why don't you let me . . . take care of you?"

Just then, Suraya heard a soft voice whisper in her ear. A familiar voice. Hussein's voice.

"Run," it said.

She didn't wait to be told twice; she just grabbed Jing's hand and began to run, thinking of nothing but the roaring in her ears, the feel of Jing's skin against hers, the way her feet felt as they thudded rhythmically against the pavement, and the very, very important fact that there were no answering thuds behind them.

"What if he . . ."

"Don't look back."

They scrambled into the back of an old red-and-white taxi idling by the station, panting hard. The old man who'd been nodding off behind the steering wheel sat up with a startled grunt. "Mau pergi mana?" he asked, rubbing the sleep out of his eyes with one hand.

"Uncle, can you take us to Kampung Kuala Gajah?" Suraya asked.

"HAH??" The driver stared at them, open-mouthed. "Aiyo, that one very far lah girl. More than one hour, you know? By the time I come back my wife will be waiting to whack me with a slipper."

"It's an emergency lah uncle," Jing said, fixing her best imploring look on him. "Please? We can pay you. Our . . . uh . . . our mother is sick, and we have to get to her. We're supposed to meet our father there."

"Mother? You don't look like her sister also." He sniffed.

"Please lah uncle. How will we get there without you?"

"Please, uncle," Suraya said. The sobs she'd been trying to keep down caught at her voice and put cracks in it, so that her tears threatened to come pouring through.

The driver looked at them.

Then he looked down.

Then he flung his hands up in the air. "Fine! Fine! But you know what happens when your wife tells you she is making mutton curry for dinner and you better come home and then you DON'T COME HOME?"

"What?" Jing asked.

"Pray you never find out," he muttered darkly as he began to pull out. "May Lakshmi forgive me."

As the taxi began to move slowly away from the little village outside Gua Musang, Suraya turned back and looked through her marble . . .

. . . and saw the pawang struggling to move, his face contorted in a grimace of anger and confusion, as Hussein hung onto his legs for dear life.

girl

BY THE TIME the taxi dropped them off, the driver still muttering away about Lakshmi and mutton curry under his breath, night had fallen and the two girls and Pink stood quietly in the town center, taking it all in.

Kampung Kuala Gajah had two main roads that intersected, along which stood rows of tired-looking shophouses with weathered signs proclaiming their specialties in once-bright colors. The only people in sight were those manning their businesses, and even those were few and far between; the man in the shop proclaiming Photostat, Printing, Binding, Laminating, We Take Passport Photo Also was struggling to bring down the metal shutters and close up, and the aunty presiding behind rows of plump white steamed pau was engrossed in a telenovela playing on her phone, squinting so she could read the subtitles. "Aiyah!" they heard her mutter under her breath from time to time, or, "Wah, like that also can!" Everything else was already closed, and the streetlights themselves seemed dim and hopeless.

"This is where my grandmother lived?" Suraya wrinkled her nose as she took it all in.

Pink shrugged his little grasshopper shoulders. *The witch wanted to live unnoticed. What better way than to lay down roots here, a town that is perpetually a stop and never the destination?*

Jing was surveying the contents of her wallet, a resigned look on her face. They'd stopped at a gas station so she could get some money from the ATM there with the debit card her mother had given her for emergencies, one she'd kept hidden at the bottom of her shoe. They'd had no choice; the taxi had to be paid for somehow. "That's it," she said sadly. "It's only a matter of time before my mother thinks to check the card activity, and then I'm basically dead."

Suraya slung her arm over her friend's shoulder. "Then we'd better make this count."

It didn't take long to find the witch's house, just down the street from the mosque. It was a small, solidly built wooden house with a green tin roof, fat mosquitoes buzzing around jambu trees so weighed down with unpicked fruit that their boughs dipped toward the ground, and just behind the house, a perfectly round pond, its surface barely visible beneath a thick layer of fuzzy green scum. It had also clearly not been occupied since the witch had died; the door was falling off its hinges, and when Suraya peeked inside, she saw cobwebs stretching from corner to corner.

This is it, Pink said, his voice low. *This is the house where the witch died.*

In the darkness, something scurried away out of sight, and Jing jumped.

"I hate rats," she whispered.

Suraya didn't like them much either, but the desire to understand the grandmother she never knew, this strange woman whose blood she shared, won out over the urge to turn and run. She pushed the door open and stepped in.

The windows were covered in a thick layer of dust, but the light from the sole street lamp outside still fought its way in, and Suraya could just make out the outlines of furniture. There wasn't much of it. The entire house was a single room, and besides a narrow bed by the window, a cupboard, and a desk with a single chair, the room was bare.

Right there, Pink said. *Right on that bed. That is where she took her last breath.*

Suraya gulped. "Has nobody lived here since my

grandmother?" In the stale, musty air, her whisper carried like a shout.

Nobody wants to live in a cursed house.

"This house is cursed?"

No. But she did a lot of cursing in it. Both kinds.

Suraya looked all around her and tried to imagine the Pink she knew here within these four walls: laughing at some silly joke she'd made, hopping onto her shoulder to get a better look at whatever she was drawing, dozing in the sun as she turned the pages of whatever book she was reading, whispering stories to her under the covers. But she couldn't. This just didn't seem like a place that was made for joy. And no matter what Pink called himself, no matter how dark a spirit he insisted he was, Suraya knew he had joy within him. She'd seen it first-hand.

Sighing, she reached into her backpack for her flashlight. Beside her, Jing coughed and coughed and coughed. "Dust in my throat," she wheezed, her eyes watering. "I'm going out-side."

"Okay," Suraya whispered. She ran her fingers along the edge of the desk, grimacing at the dust that blackened her fingertips, and opened the single drawer. Things jingled and rattled as she rummaged through—bits of broken candle, stray coins.

From the chair where he perched, Pink watched her. *Are you all right?*

"What happened?" Suraya sank down into the chair, displacing a cloud of dust that made her sneeze. "Why did my mother leave? Why didn't my grandmother try and find her? I don't understand."

If there is anything I have learned from observing humans, Pink said, *it is that families are complicated things.*

"I always wanted to know about my family," Suraya said quietly, and her voice was small and sad. "But all I've learned of my grandmother so far is that she was a horrible, mean person. And I have her blood. What does that say about me?"

It says that the most beautiful blooms come from the darkest soil.

Suraya took a deep breath to steady herself for the next question. "Do you think my mama knew? I mean, I know she knew her mother was a witch. But do you think she knew just how bad it all was?"

I do not know.

"If she knew . . ." Suraya paused, trying to find the words. "If she knew, then maybe she was just trying to protect me all along. Maybe she cares more than I thought."

She felt a gentle caress on her cheek. *It would be hard not to care about you, little one.*

"Allahu akbar, Allahu akbar . . ." The call to prayer filled the room, as clearly as if the bilal was standing in the corner bellowing it just for them.

Isyak, Pink said. *That means about three and a half hours to midnight.*

"Is that the best time to . . . to . . ." She couldn't bring herself to finish.

The full moon has powers we do not fully understand, and midnight is when it is at its peak.

"Is that a yes?"

It is as good a time as any. Perhaps you should get some rest. Pink's voice was gentle. *There is still much to do. A grave to find, a hole to dig. You will need your strength.*

"Maybe you're right."

She went outside onto the porch and sat beside Jing, who was red-eyed and sniffing and wiping her nose on her sleeve, leaving trails of snot.

Jing reached out to touch her hand. "You okay?"

Suraya took a deep breath. "I think so."

"So. Midnight, huh?"

They looked toward the mosque.

"Midnight," Suraya said. "It all happens at midnight. And we've got some homework to do before then."

"Huh?" Jing looked at her, eyebrows raised in confusion.

"Homework, at a time like this? I knew you were some kind of nerd, Sooz, but this is another level . . ."

"No lah!" Suraya punched Jing lightly in the arm. "I meant we've got to prepare ourselves. We know the pawang is looking for us too; there's no way of knowing whether he's figured out where we are or not, but we do know what he's got to work with. Whatever he throws at us—polongs, bajangs, toyols, whatever other demon he has in his service . . . we've got to be ready for them."

Jing sighed. "And my ma was so happy I'd found a nice, quiet girl to be friends with." She pulled out her phone. "All right. Tell me what I'm searching for."

"Are you sure? Won't your ma be able to find us then?"

"Better her than some monster swallowing me alive."

And as the crickets sang in the shadows and Pink watched over them, Suraya and Jing bent their heads close together and got to work.

THIRTY-TWO

ghost

The moon hung round and full and bright in the sky, but its light was often obscured by clouds, which were so billowy and ominous that they blocked out even the stars. The air was damp and heavy, that oppressive heat and humidity that promised a glorious thunderstorm. But as Pink watched Suraya wipe first one, then the other hand off carefully on her clothes, he suspected her damp palms had little to do with the temperature and everything to do with what they were about to do.

"Do we even know if this will work?" she mumbled in Jing's general direction as they walked toward the mosque, their footsteps oddly muffled by the deep, dark night.

"I find your lack of faith disturbing," Jing replied. "Also, and I hate to point this out, but . . . we don't really have any other options."

Other than my eventual enslavement by a deranged, power-hungry man, Pink added, trying to be helpful.

Suraya shot him a look. *I'll own that it's not an ideal option,* he conceded.

"Be quiet, Pink," she said, stepping carefully in the darkness, the dirt road crunching softly beneath her feet. "We have to hurry. For all we know, our moms are already on their way."

"It's not them I'm worried about, tbh."

There was a light thump, and a sharp clang that felt like it could have woken the entire village.

"What happened?"

A snuffling sound. "I tripped and stubbed my toe," Jing said. "And then I dropped the spade."

"Be careful, you klutz." With every step toward the cemetery, Pink felt Suraya's footsteps falter a little more, then a little more still. "Maybe this was a mistake. Maybe we should have tried something else."

Like what?

"I don't know. Something." There was the tiniest of pauses, then Suraya's voice in the darkness, small and sad. "I'm not sure I'm ready to lose you."

Pink's little grasshopper body felt heavy with sadness.

Nobody is ever really ready for goodbye, he said gently. *But sometimes you need to bid farewell to the things holding you back so that you can move forward.*

"You're not holding me back, Pink."

Her voice was thick with tears, and he had to swallow a sudden lump in his own throat. *You know that isn't true.*

There was silence then. In the dim light, Pink could just make out Jing next to Suraya, the too-long sleeves of her top pushed far up above her elbows, her face etched with concern. "Don't worry, Sooz. This'll work, I'm sure of it."

"I should never have listened to you." Suraya tried to mask the quiver that still lingered in her voice behind a veil of annoyance, but he heard it anyway.

"Who's more foolish?" Jing shot back. "The fool, or the fool who follows him?"

"Stop quoting Star Wars at me."

I hate to interrupt, Pink said dryly. *But we have arrived.*

The ribbons of moonlight that managed to filter through the clouds illuminated the distinctive peaks and curves of the head- and tail stones, the sharp edges of the accompanying concrete that bordered some of the graves. This was a cemetery light years from the one they'd visited before; Kuala Gajah was a tired old town, and its tiredness seeped into its burial grounds too, showing itself in the cracked, crooked headstones; the way they were carelessly scattered over the gently sloping ground, as though little thought had gone into their arrangement; the way the weeds, unkempt grass, and unswept leaves covered most of them, as though they had long been forgotten.

It seemed to Pink both unbearably sad and achingly familiar, all at the same time.

Hello, old friends, he whispered.

"Assalamualaikum, ya ahli kubur," Suraya whispered as she unlatched the little metal gate and stepped inside, her feet crunching against the dry leaves below.

"Hi, ghosts."

They both turned to glare at Jing, who hastily amended her greeting. "I mean, uh, salutations oh residents of the grave."

They stood staring at the graves spread out before them. Before, chatting with Hussein in broad daylight, the other cemetery had seemed as scary as a child's playground. Looking at this one, it was hard not to think about anything but what lay in the ground under their feet.

Suraya gripped the marble in one hand and cleared her throat conspicuously. "We should split up," she said. "Look for the graves of little kids. Like before."

"Uh-huh." Jing nodded, but didn't move. Her hand clutched her little spade like a weapon.

"It would be much faster," Suraya said. "Much more efficient."

"Uh-huh," Jing said. In the distance, thunder rumbled as though the sky itself was grumbling at their dawdling. "Or. Or, I mean. We could do it together. . . ."

"You're probably right, that's a great idea," Suraya said, speaking so fast the words tripped over themselves in their rush to be heard.

Pink said nothing. He was too busy trying to figure out exactly how he was feeling.

They set off, working their way through the cemetery methodically, from left to right. The cemetery stood on land that sloped gently upward from the mosque, so that each row was a little higher than the last. At first they tried to read each headstone that they passed, but it took too much time to decipher the looping Arabic alphabet that spelled out each one's name and parentage, and they soon resorted to eyeing the space between the headstones and their accompanying tail stones, looking for the shorter lengths that told tales of smaller bodies and younger occupants. There didn't seem to be many. The witch used to call Kuala Gajah a "stuck" town: "Stuck in time, stuck in customs, stuck in mediocrity," she'd snort. It wasn't a town where young people built a life; it was a town you moved away from while you still could, before it captured you in its web of lethargy and sucked the energy and ambition from your bones. If you died here, she'd said, you died of old age, "and sometimes your children barely make it back from their busy lives in their bustling cities in time for your burial."

Why did you come here, then? He'd asked her once.

"Because people whose lives are incredibly dull are always looking for ways to make it more exciting," she'd countered. "And will pay for that privilege."

Funny how the town had taken her too, in the end.

It seemed like they worked for a long time, moving from grave to grave in the heat of the night, when they heard it: a low, quiet humming.

Pink felt Suraya stiffen. Beside her, he saw Jing reach down to clasp her hand, hard.

"Is that . . . is that Rasa Sayang?" Jing whispered, her eyes wide.

It was. Even Pink could recognize the familiar, jaunty little tune. It was a song almost every Malaysian child grew up singing, clapping along and mouthing the words even in kindergarten.

Whoever was singing now, their voice was a low rasp. "Rasa sayang HEY, rasa sayang sayang HEY, HEYYYY lihat nona jauh rasa sayang sayang HEY!" The "heys" were expelled with joyous, enthusiastic force.

Slowly, the girls turned around.

Sitting cross-legged on the fresh mound of a nearby grave was an old uncle, wearing a thin white T-shirt and a checkered kain pelikat tied about his thin waist and stroking the wispy bits of hair that sprouted from his chin. He looked as normal as one could look sitting casually in a graveyard in the dead of night, save for one other thing: like Hussein, he wasn't quite there. You could stare straight through him and just see the faint outlines of the graves beyond.

Suraya and Jing grasped each other's hands as if they would never let go. "How come we can see him even without the marble?" Jing whispered, her voice hoarse, and Suraya glanced at Pink questioningly.

A full moon is a powerful thing, said Pink, shrugging.

"It's the moon," Suraya told Jing.

The uncle-ghost finally seemed to notice them and squinted in their direction, frowning a little. "What are you staring for?" he said, his voice loud and querulous. "You young people, staring and staring. Got no manners ah? Why so rude?"

"Sorry, uncle, sorry," Suraya stammered. "I just . . . we weren't . . . expecting anyone else to be here . . ."

"Not expecting!" He sniffed. "You come into someone's house and don't expect them to be home? What are you, grave robbers?" He eyed the spade in Jing's trembling hand suspiciously, and she quickly shoved it behind her back, out of sight.

"No, sir! We are just . . . looking for someone."

He didn't seem convinced. "Oh yes, hmm? Looking for someone? Bit late for young'ns like you to be out, isn't it? Back in my day, we made sure our children were in bed by seven o'clock."

"Wah, seven is a bit too early, right, uncle?" Jing said.

"SEVEN O'CLOCK," he bellowed. "Only way. Otherwise, whack them with the cane. Young people need DISCIPLINE." And he glowered at them as though he'd have liked to have them disciplined right then and there.

"What is all this NOISE?" From the depths of another grave, up floated another not-quite-there shape. Only this time, it was a kind-faced woman, plump as a pau and just as white in the moonlight, and clad in a worn-out kaftan with fraying bat-wing sleeves, her hair hidden beneath a ghostly knit cap. "Some of us are trying to SLEEP, Badrul."

"It's these kids," the uncle-ghost said peevishly, pointing at them. "Knocking about graves at odd hours doing Allah knows what. . . . Mangkuk. Anyway, you shouldn't waste a fine full moon night like this on sleep, Salmah."

"It's Saloma," the plump ghost said primly. "And you're right. One must not waste the magic of a full moon." She pushed strands of wispy hair from her face. "I do like a good spotlight."

"Saloma?" Suraya squinted at the plump ghost, who preened at the attention. "Like . . . the famous singer?"

"Yes!" she squealed excitedly. "Only . . . er . . . not the famous singer. But I was quite good as well!"

"Salmah," Badrul muttered under his breath. "Her name is SALMAH. And she sings like a dying cat."

"Shush," she hissed, fixing him with a stony glare. "You're one to talk, singing loud enough to wake the dead. Now, children . . . can we help you? What on earth are you doing wandering around here? This is no place for the living."

Suraya tried to swallow back her fear. "We're looking for a grave."

Badrul snorted. "Well, you're in the right place for that, I give you that much."

"A name, dear, give us a name," Saloma-or-Salmah trilled.

"We don't know the name, or even whether it's a boy or a girl. . . ."

"We just know it's a little kid," Jing supplied quickly, pushing her damp hair out of her eyes. "Are there a lot of little kids in this graveyard?"

"Going to need to get a little more specific, dear," maybe-Saloma said, shaking her head. "We've not got too many, but there are a few. Don't want to wake them if we can help it. The little darlings need their rest."

"And they're too LOUD," Badrul added.

We are looking for one who is not, said Pink, and never had his voice felt so loud, so unnatural. *We are looking for a child who does not speak. A child without a tongue.*

The two ghosts looked at each other and shook their heads. "There's only one child that fits that description," Badrul said gruffly.

Suraya's face was pale, and Pink could feel her body tremble. "Could you take us to her?"

"Him," Saloma/Salmah said quietly. "He's a boy."

"Can we see him?"

"You'd be lucky," Badrul sniffed.

"We rarely see him, dear," Saloma said gently. "He's not much for socializing, that one."

"So where's his grave anyway?" It never took Jing long to find her equilibrium again.

In answer, the two ghosts pointed.

Suraya followed the direction of their fingers up, up, up the slope to the very highest point, where the tangle of trees and vines reached out to embrace a lone head- and tail stone, its outlines just visible in the wavering moonlight.

"There," they said together.

Pink shuddered. "Pink?" Suraya whispered. "Are you all right?"

Pink looked at her, so worried, so afraid, and felt a twinge where his heart ought to be. She had been through so much because of him. Surely he could do this, for her?

Come, he said quietly. *Let us go and be done with it.*

Suraya and Jing turned to begin their trek to the grave.

And then they heard it. A frantic skittering, like the sound of a thousand scampering spiders. And a familiar voice.

"Hello, girls."

girl

SLOWLY, SURAYA TURNED around.

The pawang stood in the middle of the cemetery in his pale gray jubah, the moonlight glinting off his little round glasses. All around him, dark shapes wiggled and writhed, and Suraya recognized the creatures from the glass jars: the glinting eyes of the bajang in his civet form, hissing at them from a tree branch as he paced restlessly back and forth; the langsuir as an owl, perched on a headstone and shooting them an icy stare; the green-skinned toyol, baby face contorted into a fearsome growl, fangs bared; the tiny polongs, more than she could count, so many that they looked like one moving black mass; and others that she couldn't name and wasn't sure she even wanted to.

Fear ran an ice-cold finger up her spine, leaving a trail of goose bumps in its wake.

"Hello, girls," the pawang called out again, as if they'd just run into each other at the market. "Fancy meeting you here."

The girls said nothing. They couldn't. Fear held their throats in an icy grip, cutting off their vocal cords, making speech impossible.

The pawang tutted softly. "Ish. It's terribly rude not to respond to your elders and betters when they speak to you."

"Betters?" It was the arrogance that did it, that smug little smile. Suraya's anger bubbled inside her until it boiled over, seeping into her words, turning them loud and belligerent. "You think you're better than us just because you're older than us? Because you're 'wiser' than us? All that means is that you're an insult to your old age, because nothing I've seen from you so far makes you seem very wise at all."

"DAMN RIGHT." Jing sniffed scornfully. "In your head, you're Darth Vader. You think you're this smart villain that everyone's afraid of. You think you have all this power. But actually, to everyone else, you're Jar Jar Binks. You're just using fancy special effects to make yourself seem more important."

In the graveyard, unseen insects screeched their songs to the moon, whose light glinted off the pawang's spectacles so that it looked as if his eyes glowed.

Girls, Pink said evenly, *I applaud your speeches and*

sentiments, but I should point out that perhaps delivering them to a man who has an entire army of ghosts and monsters pointed at us is not the smartest decision you could have made.

Suraya shrugged. "It's too late now."

"Too late, indeed," the pawang agreed. "Get them."

Pink bounded from Suraya's shoulder, morphing as he went so that when he landed with a thud on the ground, it was in his true form, his claws unsheathed, a growl in his throat.

Run.

Suraya and Jing turned and ran as fast as they could, clambering over graves and tripping on gnarled tree roots in their haste to get away. "Make for the grave!" Suraya yelled at Jing, concentrating on where she placed her feet and trying very hard not to look behind her and mostly succeeding until she heard a great roar.

Then it was impossible not to look back, impossible not to watch as those tiny, monstrous shapes swarmed all over Pink, impossible not to scream as sharp claws began to rend his skin, as the pointed tips of tiny teeth began to gore his flesh.

She was still screaming when she heard a sharp *thwack*: the sound, as it turned out, of wood as it smacked against polong flesh.

There they were, rows of not-quite-there apparitions, bearing thick wooden branches and rocks picked from cemetery dirt in their barely opaque hands, and leading the charge were Saloma and Badrul, who glowered at the interlopers. "Come to my house and cause such a ruckus, will you?" he bellowed, hitching his sarong a little higher up his waist. "Bunch of thugs and hooligans! In my day ghosts knew how to behave! Mangkuk!"

"CHARGE!" Saloma trilled like an off-key diva in a B-rate opera, and the ghosts glided forward, waving their makeshift weapons and whooping and howling as they went.

"Coooooooooool," Suraya heard Jing breathe out beside her.

"Come on," she said, tugging on Jing's arm. "We have to hurry."

A crack of thunder ripped through the sky, and the rain began to fall in fat, heavy drops that fell hard and splattered wide on the ground. And then there was another sound, one that tore right through Suraya's chest so that fear spilled out and chilled her all over: a fearsome, bloodcurdling shriek. They whirled around just in time to see the langsuir burst from her owl form, a swirling figure in green robes, with long, dark hair that hung down to her ankles. Through the driving rain, Suraya could just make out her long, sharp nails and the menacing grin on her pale face as she swooped down among the ghostly melee.

"What the . . . ," Jing whispered, as they watched her swoop down on the crowd below.

"No time," Suraya said, forcing herself to turn away. "Don't look back."

The closer they got to the grave, the harder it was to hear the sounds of the battle behind them, the more the ground sloped, and the less well-tended the graves, so that they had to scramble at some points, holding out their hands to help each other over trickier bits. Jing winced as her hurt arm jostled around in its cast. The rain turned their baju kurungs into sodden, heavy nets that clung to their skin, weighed them down, and caught at their ankles; it seeped deep into the earth, turning it into thick mud that alternately made them slip and slide, or gripped their shoes and refused to let go.

It was while Jing was helping Suraya dislodge her foot from a particularly clingy mud puddle that they heard the rustling in the trees.

Suraya turned to Jing, whose eyes mirrored the panic she felt rising from her belly. "What was that?"

"I don't know," Suraya whispered back, scanning the treeline. "Maybe just a cat or something?"

"Maybe." Jing gulped. "Come on, we . . ."

But the words died on her lips because right at that moment, a shadow detached itself from the trees and slunk toward them. The bajang-civet bared his rows of sharp little teeth in a fiendish grin, staring hungrily at first Jing, then Suraya, then back again, as though trying to decide which one to devour first. And as they backed away, a snicker made them whirl around to see the toyol blocking the path behind them.

Jing looked at Suraya. "We're surrounded," she said.

Suraya nodded. "Perfect time for the plan. You ready?"

"Ready."

They turned with their backs pressed against each other, so that they each faced a monster: Suraya staring down the bajang, which had begun to hiss softly, and Jing looking straight at the toyol, who kept giggling as he advanced closer and closer to them.

"On my count," Suraya said softly.

"One . . ." Behind her, she felt Jing tense up and saw her hand slip slowly into the pocket of her backpack.

"Two . . ." The toyol's giggle turned into a cackle of glee; he was just inches away from Jing now, and the bajang was preparing to pounce.

"Three!"

Both girls moved at exactly the same time. Jing ran toward the trees, the toyol hot on her heels, and as she ran she scattered bright colored cheap plastic toys, candy, and coins that they'd cobbled together from their own pockets and from the shelves of the only 24-hour convenience store in town. The trinkets shone and glimmered in the moonlight. "A toyol, which is basically the spirit of a child, can be distracted just as a child can be distracted, with bright colors and shiny objects, toys, and sweetmeats and valuables," they'd read together earlier, and sure enough, the toyol slowed down as soon as he saw his new playthings. "Oooooooh," they heard him whisper as he sat to peruse them properly, turning each one over and over lovingly between his fingers. "Oooooooh."

Meanwhile, Suraya was trying to dodge the bajang. As she heard his quick, light steps behind her, she whirled around to face him. "You hungry?" she called out. "Here you go!" And she drew a plastic bag from her backpack and set it down at her feet before turning to run again. She knew he could send her into a fit of madness any minute now, if he could catch her. *I can't give him that chance,* she told herself, panting hard. *Please let this work. Please. Please.* Her blood thundered through her veins and in her ears so that it took a while for her to realize that she could no longer hear the bajang's steps.

She turned around cautiously and saw that he had stopped and was devouring the contents of the bag: a gallon of fresh milk and two dozen eggs they'd hurriedly purchased at a mini-mart in town once they'd read that bajangs could never pass up a meal. "Especially this one," Suraya had noted, remembering the hungry look in this particular bajang's eyes as it moved around its glass prison.

Jing caught up with her, trying to catch her own breath. "I can't believe that worked."

Suraya glanced down at the fighting down below and whatever triumph she felt quickly faded. "Don't get too comfortable," she said. "We're about to have company." For as they watched, the pawang had peeled away from the pack of fighting ghosts and was making his way up to them, his robe hitched up over his knees.

"Coming, girls!" he said, raising his voice to be heard over the thud of the rain, wiping the water from his glasses as he picked his way carefully through the graves.

Jing and Suraya looked at each other, their expressions twin masks of horror. "We're so close!" Suraya said desperately, looking up at the tiny grave at the top of the hill, just steps away. "We can make it, hurry!" She grabbed Jing's hand. "Come on!"

She turned and began to run, pulling Jing along behind her.

Jing didn't move.

"What are you doing?" Suraya turned to look at her. "Let's go!"

"I can't!" Jing said, her voice rising in panic. "What's going on? I can't move my foot!"

Suraya looked down.

In the shadow and the muck and the rain, something moved.

And then she saw it: a polong gripped Jing's foot, digging its claws into her shoes, holding her to the ground so that she couldn't lift it more than an inch. Suraya bent down to swat it away, then yelped as the creature dug its teeth into her finger and ripped out a chunk of flesh.

"You nasty thing!" she gasped, blinking back tears, blood trickling from the open wound and down her elbow, staining the sleeves of her baju kurung; in answer, the polong merely grinned at her, licking her blood from its lips with sickening relish. She tried to aim a swift, hard kick in its direction but couldn't move—more polong had come, digging their claws into her shoes and feet too, holding them flat to the ground. As she watched, more and more swarmed to them, until both her legs and Jing's were writhing masses of black, and the prickle of dozens of little claws made her bite her bottom lip in pain.

The rain stopped, as suddenly as it had begun.

"Sooz." Jing's voice was choked with fear and tears she was trying her best to hold back. "What do we do now?"

But before Suraya could answer, someone else spoke first.

"Give up, of course," the pawang said, smiling pleasantly at them from where he stood between two graves, his hands in the pockets of his sodden robe, the full moon blazing behind him, turning his face into a mask of sharp shadow and light.

girl

IF IT WERE possible for looks to kill, Suraya's dagger-filled stare would have guaranteed one more ghost in the cemetery right there and then.

"We'll never give up!" Jing said, spitting furiously in the pawang's direction. The gob of saliva landed by his foot, studded with bubbles that shone in the light of the moon, and he looked down at it with disgust.

"That's your decision, I suppose," he said smoothly. "But you're going to die tonight anyway, girly, so why waste your energy fighting it?"

"Why are you doing this?" Suraya whispered. "What do you want?"

"What do I want?" The pawang seemed genuinely surprised by this question. "My dear girl. I want what I deserve. I want the world." And he stretched out his arms wide, as if to show her just how great his claim was.

"But why do you need Pink to get it?"

The pawang shrugged. "I guess I don't need him, exactly. I just want him. You know how it is, when you collect things— you don't feel like you're really done unless you have everything. Like Pokémon! Gotta catch 'em all. . . ." He hummed tunelessly to himself.

"You're insane."

"Call me whatever you like." He smiled at her. "You're still the ones all tied up and at my mercy." He chuckled and rubbed his hands together. "Oooh, I'm so excited! I've been after a pelesit for so long! They're so much more difficult to come by. The timing has to be just right. Bajangs, toyols, those are a little irritating to handle, but doable, you know? And polong, boy, those are easier still! You just need the blood of a murdered man. And nobody notices one less vagrant, one less drug addict, one less drain on society."

Suraya felt a wave of nausea wash over her. "You . . . you killed people?"

He waved his hand dismissively. "I helped clean up the streets. I did the authorities a service, in fact. They should thank me. But the thing is, while the polong do what they're told, they have no . . . finesse. Send them to exact revenge on my enemies and people just wind up dead. And I don't particularly mind that, but it's just such a mess, and eventually people do notice when dead bodies start turning up. . . ."

"So what do you want Pink for?"

The pawang stared up at the moon. "When the pelesit and the polong work in tandem . . . oh dear girl. The possibilities are endless. The pelesit, you see, goes first. He may spread a little disease and disorder in the beginning to set the scene. And then he uses that sharp little tail end of his to dig a path into a human, so that my little polong can burrow their way inside, giving me control. Total control." He shivered in delight at the thought. "Possession. Imagine all that I could do with that kind of power. Leaders of nations would be on their knees before me! Banks would willingly offer up their riches!" He sighed happily. "The world, as they say, would be my oyster. And I do love a good oyster." His tongue flickered out of his mouth to lick his chapped, peeling lips.

Suraya's voice shook with anger. "You could never make him do it. He would never listen to you."

"No. But he would listen to you." The pawang smiled, baring rows of perfectly straight white teeth. "You see, you're coming with me."

"No!" Jing kicked and struggled against the tiny hands that held her down. "You can't do that! You can't take her!"

"Shut her up, please," the pawang barked, and a dozen polong swarmed onto Jing's face, using their little clawed hands to press her lips firmly together, ignoring her muffled yelps of protest.

Suraya glared at him. "I'll never tell him to do what you want me to. I'd rather die."

"But that's just it. He'd rather you didn't. In fact, he'd do anything to make sure you didn't." The pawang grinned. "He'll do whatever I tell him to, as long as I keep you alive. It's the perfect plan. And if he doesn't . . . well, it's only your blood that I need, after all."

Suraya swallowed hard. She knew he was right.

"Call him."

She pressed her lips together so tight it was like she was willing them to fuse together.

"A rebel, eh?" The pawang grinned as he drew something out of the pocket of his robe and flicked his wrist deftly so that a blade whispered out of its hiding place, moonlight glinting along its razor-sharp edge. "Good for you, standing up for what you believe in."

With light, quick steps, he walked over to Jing, whose eyes

widened in terror as he used the blade to caress the line of her jaw. "Of course, one must also understand that disobedience has consequences."

His eyes never left Suraya's face.

"Are you prepared for those consequences, child?"

The blade pressed a little too close, biting into the tender flesh right at Jing's chin, making her wince. Suraya watched through her tears as blood trickled down Jing's neck.

"Look at that," the pawang said, frowning at his knife. "You've made it all dirty." And he brought the flat of the blade up to his face and licked it, from hilt to tip, so that no blood was left. He looked at Suraya again, and this time there was no hint of a smile on his face. "This is your last chance, my dear, before I add your friend to my polong collection." Each word was etched with ice. "Call. Him."

Suraya bowed her head. "Pink," she whispered brokenly. "Pink. Come to me."

In a flash he was beside her, roaring at the polong who still held her in their grasp, tearing them away by the handful and hissing through his teeth as they attacked him right back. Thick, dark liquid came oozing from his wounds as he tried to fight them off.

"Tell him to stop hurting my polong." The pawang had to raise his voice to be heard over the sounds of polong and pelesit locked in struggle. "Or you'll pay the price." The bright little blade moved, settling itself on Jing's exposed neck, tender veins ready to be sliced in one quick move.

"Stop, Pink," Suraya yelled, her throat raw with tears. "Stop!"

Pink growled, ignoring her as he continued ripping away the last of the polong that clung to her shoes and tossing them to the ground before stomping them into the thick mud with his huge feet.

Suraya drew herself up and yelled with all the strength she had left in her body. "Pink. As your master, I COMMAND YOU TO STOP. NOW."

She saw his whole body go still, even as the black creatures on him still gnawed away on his flesh.

"Good, good," the pawang said, beaming as he inspected Pink up and down like a prize he'd just won. "Nice and strong, aren't you? You'll make a good addition to my little army."

Your army? Pink's nostrils flared slightly, and his flanks gleamed, damp with sweat and slick with rain.

"Haven't you heard? You're under new management from now on."

I obey no one but my master.

"And she obeys me, so that works out just fine." The pawang leaned in close, so close that his breath misted on the scales of Pink's cheek. "We're going to get to know each other well, you and I."

He pulled back and glanced at Suraya. "Tell him to shrink. We're going to go, you and I, before people come looking for you little miscreants." He looked at Jing, trembling next to him, and sighed. "I suppose I'll have to kill this one after all. Can't have you telling tales now, can we?"

"Go grasshopper, Pink," Suraya said, trying to keep the tremble out of her voice, and in seconds he was back in his familiar form on the palm of her hand.

The pawang chuckled. "I knew it," he said, shaking his head. "I knew as soon as your mother told me about you, that you were the sort to obey. A biddable child, a child who does as she's told. A child who doesn't like to make trouble for other people. A *good girl*."

Suraya's cheeks burned. Why did he make it sound like an insult?

"The best part," the pawang continued, "the most wonderful part of it all, is that taking you won't even be that much of a hassle. Your mother, she doesn't care for you much, does she?" That slow smile, that taunting look in his eyes. Suraya could feel a hot flame of anger start to flicker in her belly.

"She probably won't miss you at all," the pawang said, still smiling that wicked smile.

The flame grew and grew, spreading from her belly to her heart, igniting her chest in a fiery explosion of rage.

"She might not even notice you're gone."

She stared straight at him, and if you looked closely, you might have seen the telltale sparks of her wrath glowing in the depths of her eyes. Luckily, the pawang was not the sort of person to pay much attention to children, or indeed, believe that their emotions carried any weight at all.

"Now you tell that monster of yours that he's only to transform on command." The pawang gestured toward the grasshopper in her hand. "Go on, now. Tell him."

Suraya looked down. Her voice, when she spoke, was low and even. "Pink. You are only to transform when I tell you to. Do you understand? When I tell you, transform."

He inclined his head very slightly. *Yes, master.*

Pink never called her master.

"Very good," the pawang said, smiling at her. "All right, come now, let's get out of here before anyone finds us. We'll take care of . . . this . . . later on," he added, curling his lip as he looked at Jing. "I don't want to get her all over my jubah. Blood is a real pain to clean off, let me tell you. The number of nice robes I've had to sacrifice over the years . . ."

"One last thing," Suraya said, and her voice was clear and strong.

The pawang cocked one eyebrow and looked down at her, his arms crossed. "Well?"

"Fortune favors the bold." And with that, she took Pink and threw him with all her might behind the pawang. "NOW, PINK!" she shouted, as she stepped forward and threw her shoulder against the pawang's stomach with all her might.

The moon had draped itself in clouds and shadow, but in the dim light, Suraya could see the small grasshopper shape of Pink transform and grow as he tumbled in midair, and when he landed it was in a crouch right behind the pawang, still stumbling from Suraya's sudden, unexpected attack, still unable to do much more than pant to try and catch his breath.

Before he could regain his balance, she shoved him again, throwing all her weight behind her shoulder, trying to make herself as heavy and strong as she could.

The pawang stepped back, tripping over Pink's low, crouching form and tumbling onto his back—straight onto a fresh grave mound.

Immediately, Pink moved to hold him down.

I cannot do this for much longer, Pink said, his breath ragged. *And as soon as he is able to speak, the polong will be all over us.*

"Hang on, Pink." Suraya ran to where she could see the

ghosts fighting with the pawang's polong army. "Badrul!" she yelled. "I need a little help!"

It seemed to take no more time than it took to blink for the ghost to glide to her side.

"You heard the lady!" he barked to the grave mound. "Give her a hand, if you please."

Nothing happened.

The pawang struggled against Pink's grip, mud seeping into the soft gray cloth of his jubah.

Suraya glanced at Badrul. "What was that supp—"

"Shush," Badrul growled. "You'll see. Children, honestly," he muttered to himself. "So impatient."

The ground moved.

"There, you see? I told you to wait."

The pawang looked down, wild-eyed. "What's happening? What . . ."

But before he could finish, hands had burst out of the dark, damp earth; cold, graying, clammy hands that reached up and around the pawang, gripping him firmly around his arms.

The pawang began to scream.

Badrul spat in disgust. "Look at him, making all that riot. Mangkuk. In my day, we took our punishments like MEN." And he hitched up his sarong from where it was starting to droop at his waist and turned to march back to the melee, swinging his tree branch merrily along.

"Quick, Pink," Suraya yelled, "make sure he can't call his creatures for help!" And Pink used his great hands to shovel dirt into the pawang's mouth so that he choked and spluttered and could say nothing, nothing at all, as those cold, cold hands drew him onto the dirt, until they heard the crack of his head on a rock, and the hands glided smoothly back into the earth they had come from.

And then there was silence.

"Is he . . . is he . . ." Jing couldn't seem to finish her sentence, and Suraya shook her head quickly so she wouldn't have to.

"No! No, of course not."

He is just stunned, Pink said. *Unconscious, he cannot give commands. He cannot harm us.*

"What do we do with him now?" Suraya looked at the pawang's still body with some distaste.

"Maybe we should ask his . . . friends," said Jing, jerking her head. For all around them, the pawang's monsters had gathered, staring silently at the body of their former master.

He was never their friend, Pink said quietly. *He was cruel. They have no loyalty to him.*

"Then maybe they should be the ones to decide his fate," Suraya said.

As soon as the words left her mouth, there was a loud skittering and a mass of polong came forward, lifted the Pawang's body, and bore it away. Behind them, the bajang and toyol slunk through the shadows.

"What will they do to him?" Suraya whispered.

They will have their way, Pink replied. *The langsuir may flee, as may the bajang and the toyol. But the polongs will set out to look for his blood in a new master. Someone somewhere is about to get a nasty surprise. . . .*

High above them, they heard the langsuir-owl screech one last time as she swooped off into the night.

THIRTY-FIVE

IN THE CEMETERY, nothing moved, not even the insects and animals that usually crept and crawled under cover of the shadows. Pink, Suraya, and Jing sat in a row, savoring the quiet and the cool night air. Suraya didn't know what was going through her friends' minds, but her own was filled with the cold dread of words like *goodbye* and *gone* and *forever*, and she couldn't shake the fear that saying anything at all would bring their inevitable parting even closer.

"Well." Jing spoke first, breaking the spell. "That was . . . quite a night."

Suraya had to smile. "Better than going to the movies, huh?"

"Definitely better."

"Better than Star Wars even?"

"Let's not go that far." Jing smiled and nudged Suraya with her shoulder. "I'll just sit here for a sec, take a breather. You guys go . . . handle your business."

Pink looked at her. *Thank you, Jing,* he said quietly.

She stared at him open-mouthed for a second. "You mean you could have just TALKED TO ME this WHOLE TIME?"

I could have. Pink shrugged. *But this is the first time I have felt that you are not just her friend . . . but also mine.*

Jing's face broke out into that familiar wide grin. "The feeling's mutual, buddy." She rubbed her nose with her thumb, narrowly missing hitting her face with the shovel she still carried. "Oh. You'll need this." She pressed it into Suraya's spare hand, clasping it tight for a moment before she let go. "So I guess . . . I guess this is goodbye."

Farewell. Pink thought for a second. *May the force be with you.*

Jing's delighted laugh rang through the cemetery as she walked away.

Suraya and Pink made their way to the little grave at the very top of the hill.

"This is it, Pink," Suraya said quietly. "We're about to find out who you really are. Are you ready?"

For a moment, he didn't answer. "You don't have to, you know," she said, all in a rush. "The pawang is gone now. We have nothing to fear. We could just . . . go back to the way things were! We could be happy again. And besides . . . there's no guarantee this will even work."

Beside her, she thought she felt his body tremble, just slightly. *You know we need to do this. Or we need to at least try.*

"But why?" She was sobbing now; she just couldn't help it. "Why can't you just stay with me?"

He laid a scaled hand against her cheek, as he'd done so many times before. *It's hard to live a life weighed down by the dead. And you need to live, Suraya.*

She didn't even try to stop the tears coursing down her cheeks, and he was quiet. Pink always did know when to give her the space to feel her feelings.

When he spoke again, his voice was firm and steady.

I am ready.

Slowly, they approached the neat little grave that sat in the shade of a flowering frangipani tree, only with dark red petals darkening to burgundy centers instead of the pure white ones with the deep yellow hearts from Suraya's garden. The grave was impossibly, sadly small, its head- and tail stone bearing small cracks and a thick layer of dust. Yet flowers crept along the edges, blooming defiantly in the midst of neglect and decay.

Suraya bent down, hesitantly sounding out the name spelled out in curling Arabic script.

IMRAN, SON OF RAHMAN AND NORAINI.

She sucked in a breath sharply. The world seemed to spin that much faster, so fast she had to sit down before she fell over.

RAHMAN. AND NORAINI.

What is it?

She took a deep breath.

"That's your name, Pink. Imran." She pointed it out to him. "And those . . ."

Those . . . ?

"Those are my parents' names."

"Suraya?"

She turned her head.

It was Mama. And standing next to her, barely visible and flickering slightly in the dying moonlight, was a ghost. A small woman, Suraya realized, Pink's words echoing in her head, round and soft with a smile that made her whole face crinkle up and her eyes disappear into two thin lines.

But there was another ghost.

And suddenly Suraya understood. She understood it all: her mother's constant aches and pains; the bow and hunch of her thin shoulders; the sorrow hiding in the depths of her eyes like crocodiles in still water, waiting to pounce; the way she held her own daughter at arm's length. Because the other ghost was with her mama; a little boy no more than two years old, with a shock of dark hair and huge eyes that sparkled with starlight and fear, who clasped his hands around her mother's neck as if he would never let go.

Her brother.

Imran.

"How did you know where to find us?"

They knelt beside Pink's grave—Imran's grave, her brother's grave; Suraya's head swirled with all this new information until it made her dizzy. The witch's ghost perched daintily on a nearby tree stump, her flowery batik sarong spreading over the roots. Her brother's ghost stared at her with wary, watchful eyes.

"Your friend's mother . . . she called me." Mama's voice didn't sound like Mama's at all; it was cracked, and small, and sad. "She said you two were nowhere to be found, that her daughter wasn't answering her phone. She said the last place she knew for sure you were was near Gua Musang. I was on my way there when she called again and said you'd gotten money from a gas station near here. Then I knew for sure where you were headed. I knew . . ." Mama swallowed. "I knew what you must have been looking for."

"Tell me everything, Mama."

She let out a weary sigh. "Your father had just died," she began, and her voice creaked like a door that hadn't been opened in a long, long time. "You were a tiny little baby, and I was exhausted. We came here, to my mother, because I thought she could help me. Help us. I should have known better."

She paused as though to collect herself. "I knew about her witching—I'd known about it for a long time—but I thought she could put that aside for once and just be there for her family. And anyway, she wasn't a very good witch."

"Excuse me!" The witch's voice was like old leaves and dry riverbeds, and it was filled with outrage.

Mama ignored her. "She tried, but all she could manage were little spells and hexes. You remember that time you insisted you were sick? You threw such a tantrum when we told you that you were perfectly well, the doctor gave you placebo pills. You thought that was what the medicine was called, when it actually wasn't medicine at all. It was fake, a little lie to make you believe you would get better. Well, that's the kind of witch your grandmother was. It made people feel good to think her little spells were actually doing what they wanted, and so they paid her money for nothing more than fake pills that made them believe they felt better."

"Hmmph." The witch sniffed. "Say what you want, but I helped people. And I made a decent living for us doing it, too."

"So . . . what happened to my brother?" Suraya was almost afraid to ask; she had to force the words out before she lost her nerve.

"He wandered into the pond and drowned one afternoon while I was sleeping next to you." She said it fast and forcefully, as if she couldn't bear the words to linger on her tongue for too long, and the little boy-ghost on her back shivered, as if he remembered the feeling of cool, cool water swirling into his lungs and pushing the air and the life out of him. "My breast was still in your mouth. The sheets were wet with milk when I woke up, my head hammering, knowing immediately that something was wrong."

Suraya's tongue felt thick and fuzzy, and her throat ached with unshed tears as she reached out to grasp her mother's hand in her own.

"I didn't hear him at all." Mama's breaths were short now, and ragged, and choked with sadness. "But he must have made some sound. Right? Surely he would have splashed, or cried, or yelled. I should have heard him." She massaged her aching shoulders, shifting the boy's weight from one side to the other as she stared up at the moon. "I blamed myself. And sometimes, because it was easier, I blamed her."

"I was meant to be watching him." The witch shook her head, the lines on her face leavened with sadness. "I don't know how he got away from me. He'd just found his feet. He was a quick one, slippery, like a tadpole swimming downstream."

"But he couldn't swim like a tadpole, could he?" There was no anger in Mama's voice; it was flat and strangely matter-of-fact. "I couldn't stand it. I couldn't stand being here, and I couldn't stand her. I left, taking you with me. I wanted another life, one where nobody knew who we were. I didn't know what she would do, didn't even suspect until Jing's mother told me you were here, back in Kuala Gajah. And then I knew. I knew what she'd done to him."

"Done to him?" The witch was indignant. "I loved that boy."

"Then why did you do what you did?" There was anger now, and so much anguish it made Suraya's heart ache and her toes curl. "Why did you make him this . . . this . . . thing? This monster?" Beside her, she felt a small quiver, and Suraya knew it hurt Pink to hear these words spill from Mama's lips so easily.

"I thought it would be a way of keeping part of him with me." The witch's voice was small, and tired, and somehow older than it had ever been. "A way of keeping him alive. I just followed the instructions. I didn't know it would make . . . this."

"You were never very good with recipes." Mama sniffed, running her sleeve under her nose to clear the snot that trailed from it. "Why didn't you just get rid of it?"

The witch looked at her, aghast. "You know how I feel about waste. It was there, and it was a perfectly good resource." She folded her hands primly in her lap. "I made full use of it . . . of him. And I became a very good witch indeed. And . . ." She coughed, and Suraya thought she caught a glimpse of something more behind that prim expression, something soft and warm and altogether more likable. "And I suppose I liked having him around. Even if he wasn't . . . the him I remembered. I liked having that piece, at least."

"I'm sorry you ever did it."

"I'm not," Suraya said quietly, but with a firmness in her

voice she didn't know she possessed. "He's the best friend I ever had. In fact, he's more than that. He's . . . he's family."

"I'm family," the witch replied testily. "And what's more, you never even come to see my grave. Young people today, honestly."

"I didn't know where your grave even was!"

The witch sniffed. "Excuses."

Suraya thought of something then, and she drew the marble out of her pocket. "Is this yours?"

There was a flash of recognition in the witch's eyes. "Gave it to her, didn't I?" She jerked her head in Mama's direction. "Sent it in the post. Told her it would help her see her boy, or her man if she wanted. Never even got a thank you note, I'll have you know." Her tone was injured.

"I locked it away," Mama said, her eyes on the grave. She ran her hand gently over his name: IMRAN, etched into the gray headstone. When she spoke again, her words were for Suraya alone. "I didn't want to see him. My grief was too much for me. To lose two people almost at once. To lose your own child. It's like losing a part of your heart. And the part that was left hurt too much, so much that I covered it in darkness and did my best to feel nothing at all." She turned to her daughter, and Suraya tried hard to see the pain in her eyes

271

without flinching. "Can you see what that might do to a person?"

The little ghost around her neck looked at Suraya, and his eyes were wide and dark and scared.

"I can see," Suraya said, stroking the thin hand she held in her own, and she could. She could see the slope of her mother's shoulders, bent not just with the weight of the phantom baby that clung to her, but the guilt that wouldn't let her go, and she chose her next words carefully. "But Mama, broken mothers raise broken daughters. Did you not see how we could have each filled the parts the other was missing? Been stronger, together?"

"I see that now," Mama whispered. "But at the time, all I could think was I had no strength left for love. I had to use it all for survival. There was nothing left."

Beside her, so still that she had almost forgotten him, Pink stirred. *It is no wonder that I love you as I do,* he said. *It is because a part of me always recognized you as my little sister.*

Slowly, he got up and stood before Suraya's mother, who seemed not at all surprised to be addressed by this scaled, horned, solemn-eyed beast. *You have been carrying this burden for a long time,* he said gently, and she nodded, looking up at him with eyes that still glistened with tears. *It does not do to cling to the dead and forget the living. Will you let me take it from you?*

It took longer this time, but after a while she nodded.

Pink reached up.

The little ghost-boy hesitated.

It is all right, Pink said quietly. *It is all right. They don't belong to us, you see. They belong to each other, just as you and I do.*

The ghost-boy thought about this for a second. Then, slowly, he unclasped his hands from around Mama's neck and let Pink lift him gently into his great, scaled arms.

Mama sobbed as if her heart would break.

Pink knelt down beside her, bowing his great horned head toward her own. *You can come and visit, the way you should with your dead,* he told her, his voice soft and warm as a hug. *And he—I—we—will always be here for you, and glad to see you. But nobody is meant to live their whole lives hanging on to ghosts. Just as he and I must let go, so must you.*

And so must I, Suraya realized, and the breath she let out was a long, shaky sigh.

Beneath the tears and the sadness, Suraya thought she saw relief flicker on Mama's face as she stared up at Pink's monstrous face and placed a trembling hand on his cheek.

"Thank you," she whispered.

No, Mama. Thank you.

The pre-dawn sky was the color of a day-old bruise, and the air filled with the steady *clink, clink, clink* of trowel against dirt.

There was little light to see by, but if you were looking carefully, you might have seen a dark, hulking shape shrink rapidly into a small one, one that looked very much like a grasshopper, on the palm of a little girl's hand.

If you had very sharp eyes indeed, you might even have seen the grasshopper place one tiny foot against the little girl's damp, tear-stained cheek. And if you strained your ears, you might have heard the words he spoke for her alone, the ones that made her close her eyes for a second and lean in close, just breathing the scent of him.

Then he slipped into the small jar she held in her other hand, and there was silence as she placed the silver lid on, screwed it tight, and placed it in the deep, dark hole she'd dug with her little trowel.

Nobody said a word as she covered the jar with the damp earth, packing it tightly so you'd never know it had been disturbed at all—not Mama; not Jing, cradling her arm in its cast; not Badrul or Salmah or even the witch, who all slowly began to fade as light stole into the cemetery.

She was sweaty and shaking by the time it was over, and her face was streaked with dirt and tears.

"It is done," Suraya whispered. "The bond is broken, and this is the end."

And as the sun rose over the cusp of the world, the ghost finally closed his eyes and died.

EPILOGUE

THERE IS A wooden house on the edge of green, green paddy fields, that rattles and shakes when the monsoon winds blow. There is a woman, tall and sometimes tired, her bun still severe, her face a little less pale; a woman whose eyes still harbor a certain sadness in their depths, but also often hold light and warmth, and shine when she smiles, and sparkle when she laughs, which these days is—well, not often, but much more than she used to. You'll have to forgive her; she is out of practice, after all.

But there is also a child.

And the child is finally, finally happy.

ACKNOWLEDGMENTS

I WAS GOING to start with my agent and editor, but truly, the first acknowledgment goes to everyone who, as a child, fed me with a steady diet of hauntings: the friends who whispered scary tales between classes, the booksellers who shoved ghost stories into my hands, the adults who used the threat of monsters to get us children to behave. Your enduring gift to me was the nightmares I'm still trying to pin down onto the page. Thanks, I guess?

Thank you to Victoria Marini, who took what I described as "my weird grasshopper ghost book" and embraced it wholeheartedly, as she does every one of my unapologetically Malaysian projects.

Thank you to Alice Jerman, who was not fazed when I had to delay our first chat by fifteen minutes because I was lost in Kyoto, and then somehow stuck around despite my incoherent emails and the ingenious pranks I kept suggesting she play on her colleagues. This book is what it is because of you and your incredible insight. I guess I can forgive you for making me take out that Ewok scene.

Thank you to the team at HarperCollins, including Jessica Berg, Gwen Morton, Alice Wang, Alison Donalty, Vaishali Nayak, and Emma Meyer, for all your hard work in turning this mess of words into an actual book, and to the amazing Anastasia Suvorova, who brought Suraya and Pink to life for the cover in the most stunning way possible.

Thank you to my crew of writer friends, especially Margaret Owen, Rebecca Mix, Casey McQuiston, SK Ali, Laura Weymouth, Karuna Riazi, Atikah Abdul Wahid, and Hamizah Adzmi, without whose DMs and WhatsApp messages I would probably still be in the pit of despair. It's hard to finish writing books down there. It's way too dark, for one thing.

Thank you to my parents, who never told me "this book is too scary for you."

Thank you to my children, Malik and Maryam, who have taught me new fears every day since they were born, but also inspire me with the courage and enthusiasm with which they face this ridiculous, terrifying, wonderful world each day.

And thank you to Umar, the one person who keeps all my nightmares and daymares at bay. I love you.